THE MYSTERY THAT IS WOMAN

RUMA CHAKRAVARTI

THE MYSTERY THAT IS WOMAN

Ashapurna Devi
through her stories

Vitasta
LET KNOWLEDGE SPREAD

Published by
Renu Kaul Verma
Vitasta Publishing Pvt Ltd
2/15, Ansari Road, Daryaganj
New Delhi - 110 002
info@vitastapublishing.com

ISBN 978-93-86473-42-4

First Edition 2019

2nd Reprint 2019

MRP ₹399

Editor: Papri Sri Raman
Cover and layout by Somesh Kumar Mishra
Printed by Vikas Computer and Printers

Contents

Publisher's Note

Ashapurna Devi was born in Calcutta (8 January 1909 – 13 July 1995) and led a fairly sheltered existence throughout her life. A staunchly traditional grandmother ensured that Ashapurna and her sisters never went to school. Ashapurna's mother Sarola Sundari came from a very enlightened family and was a great book lover and her love for the classics and story books brought light to the girls in the family. Ashapurna's father Harendra Nath Gupta was a famous artist of the time who worked for C Lazarus & Co, fine furniture makers, as a designer. Ashapurna was married to Kalidas Gupta in 1924 when she was just fifteen years old.

Ashapurna and her sisters used to compete with each other by composing and reciting poems. Ashapurna secretly sent a poem to *Sishu Sathi*, a Bengali children's magazine in

1922. Ashapurna was thirteen and her poem, 'Bairer Dak (The Call from the Outside)' was published, with a request from the editor to send in more poems and stories. Thus began the career of one of Bengal's most prolific writers, Ashapurna who went on to win the Jnanpith Award in 1976 and the Padma Shri. For her contribution as a novelist and short story writer, the Sahitya Akademi conferred its highest honour, the Sahitya Akademi Fellowship, on her in 1994. The Universities of Jabalpur, Rabindra Bharati, Burdwan and Jadavpur, all bestowed D Litt on her. Vishwa Bharati University honoured her with Deshikottama in 1989. She has written more than 3,000 stories in her life time and became one of Bengal's most-loved writers.

These stories deal largely with women and the situations they find themselves in, in different settings both urban and rural. While deeply sympathetic towards the dreams and heartache of a woman's life, Ashapurna Devi never does this at a cost to her male characters. Her feminism is neither strident nor vitriolic but her characters are treated with respect and compassion. The question, whether this writer is a feminist, can only be theoretical. She herself was a willing and successful homemaker. Her stories portray the typical Bengali woman. Wife, housewife, mother, daughter and their servitude. Her magnum opus, the trilogy *Pratham Pratishruti* (1964), *Subarnolata* (1967) and *Bakul Katha* (1974), symbolises an endless struggle for women to achieve equal rights. Even though she was not highly educated in the conventional sense and had never worked outside the home, her stories are full of wisdom. She had a great understanding of the layered complexity of the world outside the confines of the four walls of a home.

Her characters whether they are mothers and daughters or husbands and sons, always seem to be people we have seen and possibly even know in our daily lives. They are never distant or two dimensional. Even the most ordinary character is imbued with personality and serves to enrich the fabric of the story where they are found. The stories belong to simpler times but as a collection help to prove that change only affects circumstances and not human nature.

We bring to our readers this collection of period-stories with the hope that it will give them a glimpse of our immediate past, the glimpse of an 'ideal' woman and the darkness under the lamp.

Sacrilege
(Awnachaar)

The whole world disapproved of Subhas Kakima. It could not imagine that a woman could be so stony hearted.

But why just a woman, was it possible for anyone to do what she had done? When a woman commits the sort of cruelty that people think impossible of humankind without any qualms, why should people not call her names?

What can they say that will be censure enough?

My mother and my aunt came home and sat in the courtyard in a way that made me think they were trying to recover from the shock to their systems.

Subhas Kakima was not related to us and therefore there was no question of the usual restrictions imposed during a period of mourning for a death in her family. Besides, married women are apparently not meant to bathe immediately after coming from a house where there has been a death; so the two women had merely changed out of the saris they had worn outside. My father's older sister, however, had taken a quick dip in the pond before coming back.

She stood in the courtyard wringing out the end of her saree over her feet to wash them clean. She then climbed up the stairs and said in her unmistakable straightforward manner, 'Thank God! Gireenkhuro is finally at peace. He has had to deal with sorrow all his life. The only reason his sickly body lingered on was because it was not his time yet; he was dead in every other way.'

She took a silk saree from the clothes rack and began drying her head with it as she sat down near my mother.

Mother let out a sigh and said, 'I have never heard such terrible things in my entire life, sister-in-law!'

'You are a slip of a girl who got married just the other day; it is not a huge surprise that you have not heard of such things. Is there anyone in the world who has heard of such things before?'

My uncle's wife said, 'I am only trying to understand how she could do this? How did her heart not break? Not just a day or two but six whole months! To hide such news and remain calm, I cannot even think of it!'

'A heart of stone,' observed my mother.

My aunt said, 'It is only when the time is right that we finally find out what people are made of. When Subhas was here, their love for each other was something to behold. Afterwards, who knows why he even went away? My mind says, he must have sensed the evil in his wife and left her in disgust.'

I knew that the fires of such criticism would not burn out easily. They would summon every word known to them to indict the woman. They would probably only stop when they needed to do their household chores.

AFTER resting for a bit longer, I got up and left the house, undecided about what I would do.

It was a Sunday. I was meant to return to Kolkata by the night train. But I did not feel like going. I think I was more tired than usual because I had been listening to people maligning Subhas Kakima all through the day.

The monotony of rural life is such that people do not hesitate to make utmost use of any topic worth discussing. This was quite an extraordinary incident. Who knew what rites of repentance would be forced upon her afterwards.

On the way back I saw a few people discussing the death on the high platform before Dinesh Ray's house. There were three or four hurricane lanterns on the steps that had been turned down. In the darkness I could not recognise any of the people that I saw.

No one needs to burn kerosene on the nights of the bright quarter of the moon; it is enough to carry a stick to tap on the road with. But that night was different. There had been a death in the village today and it was thought best to carry a light around in the dark.

Rural folk must be able to see really well in the darkness. On seeing me, Dinesh Ray immediately called out saying, 'Who goes there? Is that Monotosh?'

I was forced to walk towards them.

He said, 'Why haven't you got a lantern with you today, my son?'

I answered, 'I have been out since the afternoon.'

'Well, sit down for a little while then. Suren will go past your house on his way back, you two can walk together; he will show you a light.'

'I won't need it', I said and made to leave but I was unable to.

Dinesh Ray said magnanimously, 'You might not need it, but I need to ensure that you do have a light. I cannot let you go in the dark. Come, sit down. I suppose you are not returning tonight then?'

'No, I will go back tomorrow.'

'Do you have a day off then on the morrow?'

'No, why should it be a holiday?'

'Then how come you stayed here tonight?'

I knew that these people would not stop questioning me even though it was clear that I did not wish to answer their queries. This was one of their characteristics.

I said, 'I didn't go because I did not feel like it.'

Dinesh Ray now smiled loftily and said, 'Yes, how can you feel any other way? You must be astounded with all the events. Have you heard what Subhas's wife has been up to?'

'Yes, I did.'

'Now I ask you: you stay in the city where you must see many new-fangled things, have you ever heard of such a thing there?'

I said politely, 'No, I have not.'

Suren Sarker cleared his throat and said, 'Did you hear her excuse? She claims it was because the old man would feel pain. She was overflowing with compassion for her father-in-law! Who is she trying to fool? I ask, how did you do it, you wretch!'

'Enough of the ways of loose women, Suren. There is nothing they cannot do. After all, if the old man did get to know of it, that would have been the end of her eating fish and dolling up. Agreed?'

I felt a sudden angry pounding inside my head.

I said, 'Well uncle, I will be off then.'

'Are you leaving in the dark?'

'Yes', and I started walking.

Dinesh Ray shouted out, 'I hope you have your sacred thread on you? Or have you sent it off to be laundered like the modern people in Kolkata? You are going to walk under trees; you will obviously not listen to reason. Do you know that the spirit of the dead do not leave their place for three days and three nights?'

As I was about to walk past the path that led under the trees I had to turn and walk in the opposite direction to my house.

IF a spirit did not stop wandering the earth for three days and nights, Gireen's ghost must have been hanging around the place. He was probably even listening to all the discussions going on.

What was happening to the spirit? Was he pleased? Did he want to shower angry curses like these village elders? Who knew what it wanted.

I had never noticed any great affection on his part for Subhas Kakima. Besides, after his son Subhas Kaka left the village for Bombay with his head filled with dreams of films, he became impossibly cantankerous and misbehaved with his daughter-in-law. Not that he was to be blamed for that.

Subhas was the one surviving son out of his six children. How was his father supposed to forgive his daughter-in-law after that son vanished? How could he not blame her for being unable to stop her husband from leaving home? How could he be pleased with her?

Their family had consisted of the old father-in-law and the young daughter-in-law. Even when he threw a heavy metal bowl full of sago and barley at her in anger, there was no one else to help or say anything.

Apparently Subhas Kaka was very regular with his

letters in the early days and even sent money a few times. But there had been no news from him for the past six or seven months.

He sent neither money nor letters. The household existed in abject poverty. She sold the little gold that she had with the help of the local women.

No one had any doubts about how Subhas Kaka must have fallen into the clutches of a temptress in Bombay.

No one ever offered any real assistance or paused to think about how they put food on the table. But their household fortunes provided a topic for discussion for people at the drop of a hat.

That a helpless woman could survive on her own, that she would not fall apart despite knowing that her husband no longer loved her, that she could talk to people with a smile on her face, all these things were hard to bear. But people still put up with all of that. But it was impossible for them to put up with what had been revealed today.

While her father-in-law's corpse still lay in the house and relatives milled about the place, Subhas Kakima had presented an envelope containing a letter to all the elders of the village. She said softly, 'Please read this. Then tell me what I am to do. Tell me if I have to perform any ceremonies as penance as well.'

I stood at one side watching as all this unfolded.

The elders picked up the letter with ill-disguised curiosity, hoping that it would offer clues to wealth that had been hidden away by the dead man.

People had barely paid heed to her words, so keen were they to read the letter.

The envelope had been opened a long time ago and everybody crowded together to read the words it contained. But what did it mean? Was this a letter or an unbearably hot coal!

The expression on the faces of the elders made those who had not yet read the letter ask them eagerly, 'What is it? What is wrong?'

Satish Kundu managed to produce a smile that was both apologetic and sarcastic at the same time as he folded the letter and placed it back in the envelope saying, 'As everyone is here anyway, I might as well come clean about this. It seems that Subhas actually died seven months ago. A friend of his informed his wife as soon as it happened but she kept this vital piece of news to herself all this time!'

The effect of this statement was like a thunderclap in the room.

Keeping the news of a death secret was nothing new. People do this sometimes, depending on the situation. But why would a wife keep her husband's death a secret? What was her reason for doing so?

A murmur broke out among the people who had gathered there.

The older women opened their eyes wide and their mouths wider as they stared in disbelief. Subhas Kakima went on gathering old medicine bottles, drinking glasses, spittoons, bed sheets and clothes that her father-in-law had used during his illness with a bland expression on her face.

Then one of the women said, 'Satish, what will this woman have to do?'

Satish Kundu said, 'That is for you all to say. I have never heard of such a thing in my sixty years on this planet – and especially knowingly. As they say, unknowingly even a snake's venom does no harm.'

Satya Pishi said, 'I can take care of the marital signs such as the bangles and the vermilion, but I feel there is a need for some rites to show repentance. Such things are unheard of! Dear child, who told you to do this?'

Subhas Kakima looked up and there was a hint of a smile as she said, 'Who would give me this sort of advice? Perhaps it was my misfortune that did it.'

'Well that may be, but why do such a thing? If you thought the letter was false, at least you should have verified it with the elders.'

'But I did not think it was false.'

'What?'

This time she paused in what she was doing and said quietly, 'I thought that Father was an old man who had suffered much in life. I wished to spare him the news of his son's passing in his final years!'

Satya Pishi ground out, 'What kind of simple-minded talk is that, child? People come with their fate already etched into their lives, how do they escape that? Did you do him any favours by pretending to have all the rights of a married woman while widowed for the past six months? Will his soul not be punished for this? Anyway, call the priest and see what he says about this business. Dear Lord! Narayan! Narayan!'

The priest Bhattacharya arrived, invoking Narayan as well. He had already heard of everything that had happened.

He proposed that as the old man was her father-in-law, it would not be right for her to wear her widow's weeds as soon as his last rites were performed. He felt it would be better to perform her husband's last rites before his father's.

She asked, 'Will any of you come with me? Will it be alright if I go by myself?'

Satya Pishi said solemnly, 'I can already see that you are not the type that needs anyone for assistance. But, I have certain responsibilities. I have gone grey doing this for so many since when I was eighteen. Come, let us go. No, you will not need a towel or any change of clothes. Dinesh, you people must get things organised here while we are gone.'

I suppose Satya Pishi was furious with the widow for not allowing her the opportunity to express suitable grief at such a momentous incident.

All this happened in the morning. I was there only because it was a Sunday.

I found that my walk away from the discussions had taken me to the dead man's house by some strange coincidence. I only noticed that night had fallen when I saw the door.

I was about to turn back after some hesitation when Poncha Kolu's young daughter came outside and asked, 'Why are you returning without coming in? Kakima sent me to ask you what it was that you wanted.'

I said, 'No I just came by. Are you staying here tonight?'

'Yes, my mother sent me. She wondered, "How will this poor woman fare on her own now that the old man is dead? Nondi, go and sleep over there tonight."'

'None of her neighbours offered to do this?'

'I do not think so.'

As we spoke, Subhas Kakima came outside. Mercifully the dim moonlight hid any changes in her appearance.

She was not much older than me or even my aunt in the real sense. I had never paid my respects to her and now I stood there feeling rather sheepish.

She asked, 'Are you not Monotosh? Why have you come at this hour?'

'I thought of coming by to check how you were doing.'

'You did well to do so, my brother.'

She smiled and said, 'Do not mind that I call you brother. I am not in the habit of using endearments such as child and so on. There is something I could not say to anyone of the village that I want to ask you – there were no funeral rites for your uncle, how does all that take place after all this time, the things must be done – can you find out from one of the priests of Kalighat in Calcutta?'

'Alright.'

'Also, what kind of penance should I be doing?'

I said angrily, 'Why? Why must you do penance?'

'But I have sinned so terribly for all this time. I have behaved like a married woman knowing full well that I had been widowed. Can my Hindu faith bear such sacrilege?'

I said solemnly, 'Do you feel that you sinned?'

'Of course! I am a Hindu woman after all. But I admit that my desire to do some good was overwhelming. I thought that I would save the old man from further grief. I was the only one who could shield him from the pain of losing a son. It was so tempting to play God. That was why I hid the arrow meant for me, just like Ravan.'

I was still furious and asked, 'Then why produce the arrow today? Have you not done enough penance, given all the insults that were flung at you today?'

She was quiet for a moment. She then said, 'You know, I am not sure. I think I should be punished; harshly. Some kind of terrible retribution for spending the past months in the garb of a wedded woman while I knew everything. One cannot be blamed for drinking snake venom but what of it when the venom is digested with full awareness? Is there not a severe punishment for that in the Scriptures?'

I had no answers for her. Suddenly the twelve-year-old Nondi spoke up, 'Brother, go home now. The villagers are not a nice bunch. Someone will see you here and spread rumours. It is getting late.'

Her words were bitter but true.

Even though I had turned bright red with shame, I could not bring myself to end the conversation so abruptly. I said, 'I have only one question; no one was unaware of how your father-in-law treated you, then why?'

She smiled this time, 'Is that even a question? Just because he threatened to crack my skull with his stick whenever he felt like, it does not mean that I would have done the same given the chance.'

'But what did people make of this?'

'What people make of things is not where a story has to end.'

'Fine. Then one more question – a bewilderment which I just cannot shake off: I am thinking, just how did you do this?'

She took some time to answer this question as well.

'I do not fully understand that either Monotosh. Where did I find the strength to do all this?'

Balcony
(Dashotto)

If they were to lie on the floor of the balcony, their heads would touch the railings at one end and their outstretched feet the railings on the other. If they turned on their side, their arms would definitely find the raised threshold that led to the balcony. It was only a sliver of space, one-and-a-half arms length by three-and-a-half arms length. It could be called a pocket edition of a balcony. But it was still worth a king's ransom! There had been no balcony in their previous house. Having this balcony was certainly a matter of great luck – more than one usually expects. Even though Shubhra usually cursed her fate day and night, standing out here silenced her impatient tongue.

Late at night, whether the moon was up or not, at dew-soaked dawn or sun-burnt midday, by the wan shade of a cloudy day or by the golden glow of late afternoon – it was always good to be here. At any time of day, during a break while working or when she felt suffocated by everything that she must do, she never forgot to be grateful for the good fortune in the matter of this balcony.

It was not just because she could see the sky and the road, not just because of the connection it allowed her to have with that other world. Another reason hid within her mind, unseen perhaps even by her subconscious.

When she came out to lean her hands lightly on the railings or managed to sit down on the cane chair that she had found elsewhere – it was only then that she felt like a real person. The Shubhra who ran the household like an automaton had this other side to her – one that was uniquely her own. In that regard there was not much difference between her and the more fortunate women who lived in the houses around her balcony.

This house was large as well. Even though Shubhra's family only rented one room and she worked mechanically for eighteen of the twenty four hours in each day, her hands roughened and her nails blunted by the constant labouring and her frame barely holding up the once beautiful body, none of this could be seen from afar. No one could see from a distance that her health was failing and that the saree she wore was much washed and that the sleeves of her blouse were embroidered with coloured threads gleaned from other older saree borders. Those privileged women could not see this from their distant balconies at all.

If she had to go closer to them or sit beside them she would probably not even be able to lift her head for shame, but from this distance, there was no risk of that and so Shubhra was able to stand tall with her head held high.

This balcony was where she displayed her personality. As if at any moment and if she so wished she could call a vendor from the street but had chosen not to, simply because she had everything. She cast a negligent uncaring eye over the mountains of petticoats, blouses, chemises and dazzling saris and boxes of lace, ribbon and cosmetics that the vendors hawked on the street. She did not have the time to waste on all that frippery. She would buy what she wanted from a proper shop.

There was no such fun in watching things from a window.

There was some loss of pride in watching the world through the gaps of thickly barred windows. One felt stupid and inconsequential.

But today even standing as she was in the darkness in the three- and-a-half feet space that could take away all her pain at other times, Shubhra was not happy. She felt very helpless, even though the houses surrounding her were all dark and she did not have to affect a particular pose, filled with dignity or cultivate a certain disinterested look and there would be no harm in letting her tears descend down her cheeks. For Shubhra had learnt that she had to give up this balcony as they had to leave this house.

The spate of sackings at Prabhat's workplace had finally caught up with him. At least the company showed some consideration and gave him an entire month's pay.

But what would happen after that?

PRABHAT had been quick to make decisions. It did not take him much time to decide on his course of action. Besides, his office had set a great example of cost cutting for him to emulate. He continued along the lines of his erstwhile employers.

The first thing he proposed to do was send Shubhra and their three children back to the village. He would find a cheap boarding house for himself while he looked for another master to slave for.

Shubhra had objected tearfully and said that she would not be able to live without him. Prabhat laughed this off saying, 'The only instance where the luxury of feeling pain at being separated can be enjoyed is when there is no lack of food on the table.'

How easy it was for men to say harsh things. How simple it was for them to be incredibly cruel. Shubhra was amazed at how quickly Prabhat had made his decision about exiling her, Neelu, Belu and the baby to the village.

But was separation from him her only reason for sadness? She was to leave behind everything dear to her –

Calcutta, this vast house, this balcony, everything – to go to the gloomy ruins of their country home.

Why? Why?

If four million people could be accommodated in this great city, why could Shubhra not expect that as well? Why should she have to leave her neatly arranged household for the want of a few rupees? Especially since they said, the streets of this city were paved with money.

No, never.

She would not be a silent witness to this unfolding drama. She would not simply give up without making an effort. She would do whatever it took to stay in this house. She did not even wish to think of such a nightmare.

If Prabhat lost his job, Shubhra would find one. And why not she asks herself? There is no shame in being a woman who has to go out and work. She would work for a living. She decides to wake up her sleeping husband by prodding him.

'Listen, I want to find some work.'

He looked at her once as if in surprise and then turned to his side. When he spoke it was in a tone of relief. He said, 'Ah! Will that day ever dawn for me? Will I ever be able to sleep peacefully knowing that things are taken care of?'

'Do not tease me!'

'Are you mad? Have I said anything to oppose you? If you find work, it will be to my benefit.'

'Well, then find me a job appropriate to my skills.'

'Me?' This time he began laughing.

'Me, find you a job?' He laughed louder.

'Okay', Shubhra was really annoyed at his mirth.

'I will find myself a job then, but do not try to stop me from taking it when that happens.'

'Stop you? Why would I do that? I will be so grateful that you have condescended to become independent of me after all this time.'

Actual harsh words are probably better than this sort of sarcasm.

Had Shubhra said that she would not depend on him anymore? She thought of responding in kind but she stopped and those words never saw the light of day. Would Prabhat even understand how hard she worked or how much she sacrificed in order to depend on him for a few daily grains of rice? Did he keep any record of that?

But she could not say any of that to him. Her upbringing and sense of propriety prevented her.

But nothing prevented Prabhat from saying, 'How far do you think you will get, with your Year Ten education? At the most, a helper in a municipal school for the poor or a cleaner in some nursing home....'

Shubhra got up and left the bedside in anger.

But it steeled her resolve to work even more.

DO not smile with such disbelief if I tell you that Shubhra

found herself a job from the Work Wanted columns of the daily newspaper. People do find jobs occasionally by looking through those, our Shubhra is an example of that.

Her work is of an unusual nature. It is not in a municipal school or in a cheap nursing home. It is not even in an office. It is in an ordinary home. Shubhra has gone from managing her own household to managing a household for another woman.

She works for a woman who has recently been struck down with paralysis. The woman held Shubhra's hands and pitiably entreated her, 'Please look after the household as your own till I am back on my feet so that my sons and their father are not too inconvenienced…'

'Till you are back on your feet…' Shubhra smiled to herself. Not a request made lightly. But the money was good; a hundred rupees.

The ten notes that Prabhat used to earn will now come home via Shubhra's labours, she thought.

It was hard to understand what Prabhat thought or what his real opinions were. He had not tried to stop her from working or begged her to stay home. He had not even said that he felt demeaned because his wife had to work for a living. All he would allow himself was a smirk accompanied by the comment that the gentleman with the sick wife had certainly killed two birds with one stone; a nurse for his wife who would certainly have charged two hundred rupees and a nursemaid for his sons for the combined price of a hundred rupees.

'Do not talk like that!' Shubhra said, blushing furiously.

'I am not lying. Anyone would say the same thing. I can hardly look people in the eye anymore as it is.'

Shubhra looked surprised at this. 'And why is that? Women are going out to work these days, are they not?'

'Working and slaving are not the same thing!'

'Well, do you want me to go and tell them in the afternoon that I am not going to work?'

'Have you lost your mind? At least it is paying for running water, the electric lights, the radio, the verandah.'

He forgot to mention that it would also pay for the rice for their meals.

Was he jealous or merely vengeful?

Fine, she would not stay in the city then. She would go off to the village with three young children to die of malaria in the dank air of its poisoned ponds.

But still....

When Prabhat left to look for job opportunities at midday, she finished her chores and stood on the verandah. Her heart sank. Was this the last time that she would stand here?

She would never see these scenes again. She would be exiled from this heaven just because of a little too much pride.

No, that could not be. She would put pride aside and do the job that was hers.

THEN on the very day that she began working, with one month's advance pay in her hands, who should visit her mistress but the wife of their neighbor, the doctor. The two women were good friends.

'Oh, you are the one who has started working here. You live opposite us don't you, in that second floor flat?'

What do you think happened then? Do you think Shubhra left immediately and went off to the village?

Why, is she mad? A hundred rupees! And all Prabhat could do is utter harsh words, which were true after all; running water, electric lights, the radio, the verandah—everything stayed.

Actually she did give up one thing – the verandah.

Shubhra never goes out there anymore. Never again.

How can she?

The world out there will look back at her with the same lack of respect that she sees in Prabhat's eyes. She barely looks up from the road as she rides a rickshaw to work these days. Her sarees are clean and ironed these days and her blouses are no longer made at home. But no one will know that now.

But then, why did she stay on in the city after all that?

A Conversation

(Ektu Kathopokathan)

'Will you stop reading your paper for a while?'

I raise my eyes and ask, 'Why? Do I have to go to the market?'

'What a thing to say. As if that's all I talk about! And when do I ever ask you to go to the markets in the evening?'

'I have made a mistake, obviously! I should have said, "to the shop". Is your family here? Do you need samosas and sweets?'

'Can you stop for a minute? This is unbearable. I came to tell you about something and you just carry on. What do you read all day in those papers, how much do they tell you? I have just witnessed something with my own eyes, something so....'

'Witnessed' and 'with my own eyes'; it seems I cannot

ignore this anymore. So, folding the paper and putting it aside, I say, 'What did you witness this time?'

'A most terrible thing!' Her voice grows mysterious to create the right atmosphere for the terror accompanying the event. 'I went to the temple in the morning after you went to work. It was a holy day, the end of the month, you know?'

'It could have been, but what happened there...?'

'That is what I am telling you, that is where it happened! I went and found the place filled with people, all talking to each other. But they were all talking in whispers; there was no noise as such. So I asked one person and then another but no one seemed to be giving me the right answer. So I pushed through the crowd till I got to the front. There I saw the reason why....'

'Just say what it was that you saw – why the long introduction?'

Well, if I don't tell you what happened how will you understand? There at the front I saw a girl, she would have been about nineteen or twenty years old. She was sitting with her head bowed, and all the people were milling around her....'

Suddenly, her voice dropped even lower. '...she is from across the border!'

'People cross the border in great numbers every day, why are you whispering about it?'

'Ah! Don't you understand?' She barely moved her lips

now. 'She is a young woman. Who knows what trials she has been through? Someone took her across forcibly.'

'Thank God she has "come back", then.'

'Of course, that is what I meant. How sad! Finally I heard the whole story. She did not want to say a thing, but everyone poked and prodded until she gave in. Then she blurted out the whole thing. Oh, how she wept as she told us, we were almost ready to cry with her. She had eight people in her family including her parents and her brothers and sisters, but she does not know what happened to them. They might have been killed or perhaps they escaped, but she was captured and then – well, you know?'

She stopped for a while, perhaps to give me a chance to imagine the events, and then said, 'That innocent child, like a flower in the hands of those monsters! You know, she is just barely alive after....'

Somberly I said, 'Since I know, there is hardly any need to go into so much detail! So what happened to the girl? Tell me, how did she manage to come here?'

'That is a very long story, quite an epic! Who knows whether it is true or all lies – she says she studied in a college, she was about to sit for an examination. Her father was a lawyer, they had a house, a car of their own but she did not tell us his name. Oh! How she cried! Even the cruelest heart of stone would melt in the face of those tears!'

'That I can see for myself! But why doubt what she says?'

'No, I was just saying… now she is pleading with everyone to give her a place to stay for a while. She does not want to go to a shelter. She is from a good family; she wants to stay with good people.'

'And, did anyone give her a place?'

'Are you nuts? Who would give such a girl room in their own home?'

'Why did you not give her shelter?'

'Me? Whatever next!'

'Why? Can we not open this house to one girl?'

'Of course, we could. But to this particular one? What is wrong with you?'

'What is the harm in that?'

'There is nothing but harm in doing this. But will you understand if I tell you?'

'Perhaps I won't, but after hearing you say, "Even the cruelest heart of stone would melt", I hoped that….'

'Why should I not feel sorry for the wretch? Why should I not shed a few tears? Not everyone is as dry and soulless as you! But feeling sorry is one thing and – there is still the matter of right and wrong and honour in this world.'

'That is true. There are no hassles in being able to feel sorry for another in pain, no money needs to change hands and as a bonus you gain a sanctimonious sense of wellbeing. Is there anything better? So, she was sent packing to a shelter in the end, was she?'

'What do you mean, packed off? Your words are enough to drive one to the grave. One of the men working at the temple, a son of the Bhattacharya family, offered to take her to the shelter.'

'Thank goodness! I was beginning to worry that someone had probably taken her in and lost face in your eyes by coming to her aid.'

'You do like mocking people. If she had been an old hag or a working class person, one might think of providing shelter. She could have stayed, looked after the household, done all the work and that would have made sense. But this girl, some college student from God knows where, some lawyer's daughter to boot, what would people do with her? As the saying goes, too hot to swallow, too good to spit out!'

'True, very true. Too good to spit out... that is a problem indeed.'

A few days later:

'Have you heard? Whatever next!'

'What?'

'Remember that girl I was telling you about, the one who escaped?'

'Yes, what has happened to her? Is she dead?'

'Dead? No sir, not at all! You might say, who did she smite? What a thing to happen! I thought I would die when I heard it.'

'This habit of giving long introductions is here to stay, I can tell!'

'What introduction? Do you remember the other day, I told you that one of the men, Mrs Bhattacharya's son, his name is Murari or Mukunda, took her to the shelter? Now I hear that he did not take her there at all! She cried so much at the name of the shelter on the way there in the car that he relented and took her to a friend's house. Imagine!'

'What a courageous friend!'

'You always confuse foolhardiness with courage. One must think of right and wrong as well. Now I hear that fellow Murari desperately wants to marry her. Oh! The shame! I could just die! Apparently she now wants to sit for her college examinations as well. Just imagine the gall! She was literally near death the other day, and now she is well enough to want to appear for examinations! Shameful!'

'But that is good isn't it? She has not allowed her experiences to destroy her….'

'What is so good about it? The fellow is running around trying to organise her enrolment. There is no accounting for taste these days. Men see a little beauty and fall under its spell. Otherwise, that violated girl, God only knows what happened to her before! Dear God! Durga! Durga!'

'But once upon a time, we Bengalis knew words such as "compassion" and even "pity"….'

'Compassion? Pity? Whatever! Anything else you would like to add? Just as I had said: she is a college girl, she knows all kinds of tricks and has cast her spell on the young man! I am just thinking of his mother's plight. Such a good family and to suffer such a black mark! She was so proud, now she has been well exposed to everyone! She must be crying her eyes out. How can a son be such an enemy? If he wanted to help her, he should have done it quietly in his own way. And what kind of a marriage is this anyway? Trying to pull the wool over everyone's eyes! What else can it be?'

'That is what I feel too. I truly envy him.'

'What? Well, why feel envious? You can go and see if you can do the same thing. You may not find a fresh one, but surely a widow or some used up woman must be out there waiting for you!'

'No, my time is gone.'

'You are really sad, aren't you? Wait, your time is almost upon us. There will be no rules to follow very soon. This boy is a Brahmin and that creature is from the lower Kayastha caste, a Mitra apparently. Even so they are getting married, are they not? They are having a Hindu ceremony too. What will amaze you even more: the date is at the end of this month, even though there are no suitable days according to the calendar. How Hindu is that?'

I shake my head, mortified.

The month of Chaitra! How Hindu is that?

Perhaps this is the rule.

It is wrong to criticise one person. People will never understand what it means to feel suffocated until the blow lands on their own heart.

We can flood the world with torrents of 'Oohs' and 'Aahs', we can light fires with the heat of our pens, our meetings and our petitions. In some cases, we are even prepared to take to task the over-tasked leaders at our helm. But when the storm comes to our doors, we close them with fanfare and sit down to count our prayer beads and calculate what losses we might suffer. If shutting one's eyes means freedom from all fear, why open them at all?

Brahmins and Kayasthas; Phalgun, with its suitable days and Chaitra with none.

These questions are still alive and well.

Amazing!

But then again, perhaps this is only right. This is how our orthodox religion managed to send its roots so deep over the ages.

But will they continue to do so?

If drowning people do not accept their inevitable decline into the abyss and instead claw at the banks to save themselves, won't the land crumble away with them gradually?

A House Of One's Own

(Paka Ghor)

It is a small two storied house of flimsy construction. It looks new after a recent paint job. The pale pink walls with dark green doors and windows set into them and red Ranigunge tiles over the verandah; all these make the house look picture perfect when seen from a distance.

It is hard to imagine the house in its early days from what you see now, just as it is difficult to look at a fully clothed grown man and imagine the form he had within his mother's womb.

When the house was first built, it was one storey high. Even though the walls were cemented firmly to the foundations there was no money left to make the roof solid. Corrugated tin sheets were laid across the walls to make do.

Monotosh and Mohitosh were brothers who had left

the ancestral village with their wives to move to Kolkata. There they bought a tiny piece of land at one end of the city and built a house with two tin roofed rooms for themselves.

Even though the roof was of tin, it was a house in the city; and not just in any old city, it was in the city of Kolkata. There was water available from the tube well whenever one wanted. Electric lights with a switch to turn them on were not as common then. That celestial glow was meant only for the homes of those with money lining their pockets.

But that was of little consequence; kerosene lamps were no less a sign of affluence, were they? The house was a palace compared to the ones in the village with their straw thatched roofs and mud walls. The brothers were happy, and their wives were grateful.

Those were not mere rooms of brick and cement, they were heaven. They could never have enough of looking at them, when they treaded on their own cement floors their hearts burst with pride. Once two more rooms were raised on the spare land left at the back, there would be nothing more to want in the whole wide world.

Monotosh's wife Padmo was older and had no children. Her younger sister-in-law Champa had a boy and a girl. But Padmo did not mind that at all and outsiders would, in fact, have been hard pressed to tell who their real mother was. Do you think the children themselves had any idea?

They actually found it easier to request their aunt Baroma for those little necessities of childhood.

The two brothers were united at heart; their wives were the best of friends.

It was a joy to see the household.

Two bedrooms, a lean to kitchen to the side; even though the two sisters-in-law spent most of their time in the lean-to, their hearts swelled in the happiness of the brick walled rooms. Those filled up gradually with bits of furniture and childish fancies.

The brothers had moved to the city to make money and they were out all day at markets and shops. From there they brought back things for the house.

Sometimes it would be Monotosh buying two cheap mirrors, telling Padmo, 'Here, look at yourself as much as you want! Remember to hang one in our younger daughter-in-law's room.' He called her Choto Bouma after the old fashion.

Another day it would be the younger brother Mohitosh with two pairs of terracotta birds. He would go to Padmo's room and ask, 'Which wall do you think these will look good on?'

Monotosh would bring home little frocks, pinafores, coats and pants; Mohitosh would buy a pair of saris, combs and a couple of soaps.

Mohitosh once brought a shawl home, saying, 'Brother, use this one and throw away the old faded one you have. It is really quite shameful!'

Monotosh tried to return it protesting, 'You are the one who has to attend important gatherings. I have been telling you to get a warm coat for yourself and now you spend good money on trivial things! I am fine, I tell you.'

Why do such ideal days not go on forever?

THE first cracks showed when they got tradesmen to fix up the house for the first time. There were some savings from the business and Monotosh said, 'Let us add two more rooms.'

Mohitosh disagreed, 'No! We must have a proper roof done first!'

Monotosh had his reasons – the house was filling up with their possessions, the rooms were needed sorely. Mohitosh had a good reason for saying what he did too – little would be achieved by adding more tin roofed rooms.

Needless to say, Mohitosh won this round with the support of his sister-in-law. He had the support of his own wife Champa as well, but her wishes were always voiced in private. Both women dreamed of going upstairs on the terrace to dry their hair after bathing, to make lentil dumplings or bori, to preserve jars of pickles and to lean over the sides like the other wives of the neighbourhood and watch the world and all that was in it. They had come to believe that their lives were somewhat incomplete without the presence of a roof terrace. They were conscious of this shortfall, setting them apart from their more fortunate neighbours.

They were not particularly close to any of these women, something they felt keenly as village women. But how would that be? One does not become a neighbour simply by living next door to each other. Will the grass at its feet ever become neighbour to a mighty peepul fig?

The savings went into making a proper roof terrace and stairs to go upstairs.

Everyone was happy, that is everyone but the older brother. He never went up to the roof once, saying he became breathless when climbing stairs. He also increased the frequency of his complaints about the lack of space in the two rooms whenever he could.

THE second time that they had to get tradesmen in was also the time when the crack widened from a hairline fracture to an actual rift.

Mohitosh wanted to add on a second floor. This would solve the question of the shortage of rooms. The spare land would not go to waste either for the corrugated tin sheets from the old roof could be used over a trio of single brick rooms, their un-plastered walls containing the kitchen, a storeroom and a bathroom. When their wives were younger, they had not thought this necessary as the tap in the yard had done well enough for all such needs. Their men just had to stay indoors and out of sight at certain times of the day. It was never a problem. These days, it was a real worry when one of the women wanted to bathe. Some unwanted stuff that had nowhere else to go was also piled on the old kitchen roof; tins with leaks, broken flower pots, bamboo scaffolding, ropes of coconut fibre. Even some leftover sand and powdered lime made its way to the place.

Monotosh was not pleased this time either.

His reason was not very practical as he thought that having a second floor would invite the jealousy of their neighbours. What a thing to say!

Mohitosh said, 'But that is one of the very reasons why one builds a house!'

Eventually his word was upheld and truckloads of bricks, rubble, lime and cement came to the house, much to the jealousy of the neighbours. There were also huge iron beams, concrete frames and wooden shutters for the windows.

Mohitosh supervised everything with great enthusiasm while Monotosh sat implacably and smoked tobacco. When the tradesmen came to ask him about things because Mohi was not at home, he said, 'Ask him when he is back, I am not really the one to know.'

Padmo tried to reason with him at times saying, 'Why are you acting this way? What will your brother think? What will our younger daughter-in-law feel if she hears you?'

Monotosh replied, 'Why should they make anything out of this? I just tell them to go to the one who is paying for everything.'

This was not untrue as it really was Mohitosh's money as he had been playing the share market recently. The tamarind supply business that the two had started did not appeal to him anymore and he was even heard saying that he felt ashamed to say what the business dealt in.

Monotosh objected to moving rooms after the second floor was completed, saying that he did not need to have a room upstairs. He had never used stairs in his life and was not going to start in his old age. He was fine in his downstairs room. But this strange whim of his was not to last very long. Padmo had not lost all touch with sanity just because her husband had lost his head. It had always been decided that the two women would have the two upper floor rooms but clever Padmo gave her younger sister-in-law the better room to the south. Downstairs it had been the opposite; they had taken the airier room to the south as 'the elder gets the better share.' But at that time, Monotosh had contributed equally whereas this time he had remained a bystander.

But Padmo staying upstairs while Monotosh stayed downstairs was not a system that was going to be successful for long either. Soon he was sleeping upstairs too, his face clouded with anger and his temper stretched to breaking point.

This time Mohi organised the housewarming, the grihapravesh, with some extra pomp.

It was summer. Monotosh lay awake at night fanning himself and tersely said, 'I spit on such a room, what kind of room is it without a window to the south! Better to sleep in a cowshed. What bliss have I achieved by sleeping on the second floor?'

Champa's daughter had always slept with her aunt and that had continued after the move upstairs. She must have been sleeping lightly in the heat as well and in the morning she gave her mother a detailed account of the night's conversation. After all she was older now, old enough to know who her real mother was.

Champa raised the subject as she chopped the vegetables, 'Sister, if Elder brother-in-law is feeling unhappy about the choice of room, let us change over now.'

Padmo, startled, answered, 'What kind of talk is that chotobou? Are an old codger's likes and dislikes so important?'

'Only you can answer that Sister, but seeing that he has slept in the best room all his life, he could be having a hard time now. We have, after all, spent half our lives in a stuffy room – have we ever said a single word?'

Needless to say, the gracious offer that Champa made was not matched by a corresponding tone of unflinching respect in her voice.

Padmo was mortified. She tried to lighten the mood

by giving various examples of her husband's lack of understanding. But she rained curses on Champa's daughter Chandana. All in silence of course, as she said to herself, 'How could she be any better? As they say, the bitter gourd is bitter all over whether you taste its fruit or its leaves! After all, just look at the mother she has!'

The house-warming was done in a hurry but the house was not decorated yet.

Childless Padmo was never too tired to work and she carefully dusted and brought all their things upstairs. She hung them on the brand new walls; faded dusty terracotta fish, birds, pigeons; pairs of each. Mohitosh always bought two of each. Padmo had many things she had bought as well – that she had lovingly brought back from each Ratha, Dol and Rash fair she had visited throughout her life. She had brocade tapestries, mythological figures made of glass and porcelain angels; she had tin plaques, pith flowers of shoal and wooden boxes. She had made many decorative items too, working painstakingly to embroider flowering plants in wool, glue fish scales into baskets and melt wax into toys.

She had collected these all her life. She spend a long time and thought at length before placing each in the best place possible. She was then slightly ashamed, for even though Champa may be lazy, she deserved to have a neat room too. With that thought in mind, the next day she sat down to clean the dust off Champa's knickknacks.

Champa had been sleeping upstairs in the afternoon; she came downstairs to get her son's feed, saw Padmo and said with a smirk, 'What are you doing now!'

Padmo replied enthusiastically, 'I did the other room yesterday and I will finish these today.'

Champa smiled sarcastically and said, 'Dear heavens no! There is no need to drag all that ugly stuff and fill the room upstairs. They will stick out like bad teeth! "He" has promised me a set of pottery dolls and a couple of good paintings.'

Padmo shrank within herself and said rather stupidly, 'What of these then?'

Champa laughed out loudly and said, 'What do you think? Is anyone taking my room downstairs away from me? Let those stay there, the children can play with them without worrying too much if they do break them. But old things in a new room? Absolutely not! My stomach turns even to think about it!'

She emphasised her final words.

Padmo felt as if she had been shamed in public and had nowhere to hide.

Only the gods knew how she put her work down and managed to come away.

Their old bed was still sitting in the middle of their downstairs room, as it had not been allowed upstairs, thanks to Mohi's fear of damaging the wall of the stairwell. That was the sole witness to her tears.

Why had Champa not said anything yesterday? It must have been on purpose!

How she must have laughed to herself and smirked as she told her husband! She must have spun such a tale of how carefully Padmo carried all the old rubbish upstairs and decorated her new room. She must have enjoyed the spectacle of the 'things sticking out like bad teeth' on the white washed walls of Padmo's new room and kept quiet about everything.

Today there was no way of getting rid of them. That would give her even more reasons to laugh. But would Padmo have thrown anything away, even if she did have the chance? All the memories saved up throughout her life! Is Champa not a woman too? Did the gods not give her a heart? Or did they forget to supply her with that thing called compassion? When she got up after shedding many tears in the afternoon, recalling that it was time for the cooking fires to be lit, she was not angry with Champa anymore but her heart was filled with an unquenchable sense of betrayal by her husband which reared itself in anger. Was Mohi the only one to spot 'pottery dolls'? Did Monotosh not have the money to buy a couple of 'good paintings'?

Ever since the tamarind business started failing, Monotosh had become like a soldier at war time; Even Padmo found it difficult to be in his company.

ARRANGEMENTS for Chandana's marriage started when she was of the right age.

Mohitosh went to meet the families of prospective grooms in secret, letting only Champa know about his trips. He had got an idea in his head that the older couple would do something to obstruct the arrangements.

Padmo did not understand this initially, and used to question him relentlessly about their plans for Chandana. She had no idea that it was alright for her to not worry about Chandana's future well-being. The first inkling of what was really happening came from Champa's irritability. Mohitosh had been avoiding her direct questions, answering as vaguely as he could when Champa suddenly burst out from beneath her veiled head, 'Surely the marriage will not take place without the world knowing about it, everyone will see and everyone will hear! I don't understand all this curiosity! Why, I never feel like poking my nose into other people's business, do I?'

Padmo understood where she stood from that day and learned to curb her desire to poke her nose in other people's business. But eventually, when the marriage did take place in plain view of the whole world, she 'saw so much', 'heard so much' and did so much that she took to her bed with the fever.

Whenever a room is left empty, rubbish tends to be dumped in it.

All the unwanted flotsam of the household had come to gradually find their way to Padmo's old room downstairs.

One day Mohitosh seemed to notice the state of the room for the first time. He shouted loudly at no one in particular and threw away broken baskets, tins for storing fuel and the coal pot. He kicked away the bundle of clothes that Padmo had been saving to exchange for steel utensils and then declared, 'This room must be emptied right away, Chitu's new tutor will need a room to teach him in!'

At first Chittotosh used to sit on the bare floor on a grass mat while he was studying. Then came a cheap table, tin chairs and an old bookshelf bought at an auction.

The old lean-to had been strengthened with two posts; all the stuff from the room went there. This time Padmo's old bed was dispatched there too – the bed that she had shared with her husband for twelve years; well, not that there was much harm in that. The lean-to was after all the airiest space. Padmo used to come downstairs from the heat and lie down there, now she had the bed to make herself comfortable.

When a daughter is married, a son-in-law arrives; when he arrives it is not enough to just give him a meal, he must also be offered a chance to rest and thus a room is needed. Champa had given birth to another girl and could hardly be expected to be shifting with all the baby's things, each time her married daughter visited. It became inevitable that Padmo and Monotosh must then move.

Every night they had to find shelter in Chitu's study room.

When she left her own bed and came downstairs, Padmo felt a strange suppressed pain burning her up; when she lay on the floor and looked up at the ceiling she no longer saw how it once was, the tin roof and her beloved things on its walls. The room where she once felt heavenly happiness; the one which she could never grow tired of looking at. She truly did not remember those times.

Her mind filled with the insult of having to bring her elderly husband downstairs each day. Yet she could not bring herself to say anything about this for shame. How could she, now that he was completely idle and homebound these days.

THE tug-of-war had been daily. Then one day, the tugging stopped and the war became the only reality.

Monotosh came home from the markets and passed away within a few hours, possibly from the effects of a heat stroke, giving up his rights to the upstairs room for ever. Towards the end, despite all his utterances to the contrary, he had come to feel a strange attachment for the room.

Padmo herself declared that she did not wish to have the upstairs room any more.

Many of the neighbouring houses were visible from its windows and she had even befriended a few of their inhabitants while going up and down the stairs; what would they say on seeing her bereft white saree-wearing appearance? How would she wander about like a ghost of her former self before their curious eyes?

It was quite possible that they would have had to relinquish the room even if this disaster had not befallen her. Chandana came to her parents to have her baby and stayed on for about a year. Where would she have stayed apart from this room?

Around this time, Mohitosh engaged tradesmen once again. This time the house was re-plastered and electric lights were installed.

The threadbare remains of Padmo's old dolls were dumped in baskets. One by one, they were given a fitting farewell in the caring hands of Champa's younger daughter Anjana.

But who was caring for Padmo?

It is not possible to stay on in Chitu's study room. He went to college now and had friends who visited him constantly. He has organised the space well with couches and tables. The other room on the ground floor was Mohitosh's sitting room. He was after all the head of the household now and must have a room of his own to sit in.

Where would Padmo go then?

The answer came from Chandana who said, 'Aunt can easily live in the storeroom. I don't even understand why a single widowed woman should need one entire room to herself any way! In my in-laws' house my aunt-in-law lives in the storeroom at the front. There will be some problems, of course! Who can expect to live in luxury eternally?'

Chitu hesitated, saying, 'But in the storeroom?'

Chandana retorted, 'Why, what is wrong with it? It might have a tin roof, but the walls are plastered. Even these rooms used to have corrugated roofs once. Do you not remember?'

Of course he did. He remembered being deafened by the sound of the tin being removed. Hence he was rid of his hesitation, his conscience pricked him no more.

Padmo took up residence in the storeroom. The old bed was brought in from the lean-to. It had lost one leg and was propped up with a couple of brand new bricks.

She lit an old clay oven in one corner to cook herself some boiled rice and vegetables and she slept on the bed. Her health was very poor and she could do nothing for the household.

A Brahmin cook worked in the kitchen; Champa came to the storeroom one day to get ingredients and quite possibly addressed her remarks to the sky as she said, 'Like a thief in my own home – that is now my state! Half-dead with exhaustion and I still have to put up with this VIP and feed and clothe her daily. Has she no shame? How can she just eat and sleep and do nothing else the whole day – I will never understand this kind of nature! Is it true then, what they say about splitting a jackfruit open on someone else's head to eat its sweet insides? Amazing!'

They do not have to clothe her and feed her for very long. First the food stops, then the rest....

Due to a very long drawn fever Padmo had to be removed from the storeroom. Who knew what was making her sick!

The lean-to was made livable with a couple of new posts and the rubbish moved to a side to make a little space. Where she had once sat with her sister-in-law Champa with plates of rice, competing with each other in eating drumsticks and fish tails was where Padmo was to end her days.

THE house was repainted to erase the traces of Padmo's illness. Mohitosh then started to prepare for his son's marriage.

This was the son who had brought glory to the family. No one in his family had ever graduated from college. His wife obviously had to be selected after much careful searching.

Mohitosh managed to do just that. He found his son a wife without a single fault. She brought so much wealth with her by way of dowry that the neighbours were stunned by the display. And why not, I ask? After all, Jyotsna's father had never had a graduate son-in-law before this.

It is not as if Padmo's name did not come up once or twice during the festivities, but she was not really missed as she had ceased being useful for a long time. She had kept aside one of her good gold jewellery pieces for Chitu's bride and had left this with Champa before passing away.

Champa gave her daughter-in-law the heavy old fashioned necklace and said, 'Daughter, you had an aunt-in-law. She left you this as a blessing before she died.'

Jyotsna took one look at the design, shrank in horror mentally and decided that she would have it melted down to make a neckpiece in the modern Metro design, that was one thing she had not been given by her father.

The new bride was a wealthy man's daughter and Champa was filled with hopes. She gave up her spacious airy room to her son and his wife and moved into the room where there were no windows to the south.

Mohitosh did not have to complain about the lack of a breeze for he had already bought electric fans on the occasion of his son's marriage.

Chitu was the one who complained.

He said, 'Ma, you must remove your heavy dresser from that room, I feel suffocated.'

That dresser was the most expensive piece of furniture in Champa's room. She clapped her hand to her face and said in wonder, 'What, that is a piece of English furniture; it cost well over a hundred and fifty rupees!'

'You can hang your expensive stuff around your neck, Ma. I just have to look at it and I feel hemmed in.'

'But how about the daughter putting her good saris in the....'

Chitu interrupted her hurriedly, 'We don't have to worry about that! Her father is eager to give us all the furniture we can have. He was saying to me the other day, his daughter has always liked good furniture but he cannot do anything about it because there is no space in our house.'

Therefore – space must be made. A truck arrived loaded with furniture from Jyotsna's father's house; a bed, wardrobes, a dressing table, chairs and much, much more. Everything was in the latest Metro design, shiny and sleek.

Champa's English dresser, her big four poster bed and her heavy armchairs seemed to hang their heads in shame.

The things that come from her son's in-laws were rightfully her property too. It was only because he was such a good catch that he was given such respect but she still could not feel completely happy at the turn of affairs. She felt a great disenchantment with Mohitosh. Look at all this modern stuff – why did he still have such old-fashioned tastes. It was not as if he bought things on the cheap, in fact he spent thousands on ornate junk. The few things that they had made it hard to move around the room, and now it is so much bigger despite all of Jyotsna's furniture in it.

CHANDANA had gone home after the wedding but she now came back to help the new bride settle in. Champa began to sleep in the sitting room with her two daughters and her grandson. All of them could not have slept in the bedroom with Mohitosh. He needed to rest and to sleep. Besides, the fan was on all night in his room and that would cause Chandana's son to catch a chill.

Jyotsna looked after her father-in-law and kept his bedroom tidy. Mohitosh seemed to want no one else and was completely enchanted by his daughter-in-law. Champa felt a strange sense of jealousy seep through her veins and her nerves, she could not express this and hence she could never be very pleased with her daughter-in-law. Chandana found much wrong with her brother's wife as well; failing to see anything lacking in her looks, she found fault in her qualities.

Jyotsna did not particularly care about what they thought; she had anchored herself to the one who mattered.

'When Chandana leaves, the house feels so empty. Her son fills the house with his antics.' Mohitosh expressed a secret desire – 'Won't it be nice if Chitu has a son?'

Champa could not hold back her annoyance, she said, 'Don't say such things! They have not been married a full year yet!'

Mohitosh felt embarrassed. But he still craved the babbling of a little child in the house.

Perhaps it was not fulfilled because he wanted it so much.

Within a year of Chitu's marriage Mohitosh died after a fever that lasted three days. The child was yet to arrive. Jyotsna was with her parents for the duration of the pregnancy.

She came back six months later with her daughter.

It was hard to say what would have happened if the

child was a boy but Champa could not bear the sight of the girl. She thought the child was unlucky. Jyotsna did not take long to figure this out but she was soft spoken and said little. Her former protector gone, she now took matters in her own hands.

Despite their prosperity, Chandana did not have a happy relationship with her in-laws as her mother-in-law was shrewish and strong-willed. She was used to staying in this house most of the time but Jyotsna soon put an end to that. Only she knew how she managed this.

After her daughter left, Champa felt somewhat alone and friendless. She felt that her power over the household was eroding from within. There were signs of this everywhere.

Chitu one day told her, 'Ma, I am buying a radio.'

She was amazed and asked, 'What? What did you say you will buy?' She did not know this word yet.

'A radio', Chitu explained to her in detail. 'Is like a gramophone….'

Champa said gloomily, 'What do you need that for, do not buy it. Your father had wanted to buy one all his life. All he did his whole life was work for the house and his family!'

Chitu said sheepishly, 'No, it is not the same thing, it is something else. It does play songs but not on records.'

'But still, they are songs? What will the neighbours say if they hear us playing songs at this time of bereavement?'

Suddenly Jyotsna interjected, 'Then all the fun and music of the city should be banned! Is there any house where there has not been a bereavement Mother?'

She had never spoken to her mother-in-law previously in her husband's presence.

Champa looked on in amazement. She forgot to rebuke her.

Chitu left with a sulky face. People went about their business in silence, ignoring each other for the next few days. Eventually on the day that Champa herself thought of telling her daughter Anjana to tell her brother to buy the gramophone, Chitu returned home in a taxi with a new radio set.

Whatever its appearance, Champa could not tell its difference from a gramophone.

Poems, songs, devotional hymns – all these played on it, just like a gramophone.

Next to arrive was a swinging crib for the baby and a sewing machine for her mother. Jyotsna brought her own childhood books, her toys and her harmonium. They did not fit into one room. Chitu raised the subject via Anjana one day. Did Champa need her upstairs room anymore? She was elderly and must find it hard to climb the stairs. She could easily live in Chitu's old study room with Anjana, as Chitu now used his father's old sitting room.

THE English dresser, the four poster bed and the chest full of utensils all move downstairs with Champa to Padmo's old room. The bed stays unassembled as there is no space for it. Many of the necessities of the household were slowly becoming superfluous. What one saved one day becomes rubbish the next. The things that were no longer in use but could not be thrown away were the things that made their home in this room.

In the meantime, Anjana's wedding was held without much fanfare. How was Chitu to spend a lot if even the wealthy were not doing that anymore? There was no question of inviting the new son-in-law to a meal. It was hard to organise a meal befitting the occasion and even harder to spare the space needed to host him for the night. Where was the space?

Then the Fifties arrived and all one heard was independence, poverty and evil times. The results of independence arrived in the shape of refugees. The people who had houses were fortunate indeed. Even the one who had just a room to spare was about to become as rich as a king.

Chitu raised the subject after a convoluted discussion about need and poverty. The two rooms downstairs could fetch a minimum of seventy rupees easily if rented out. Someone at his workplace had been pressing him. How much better for the family to have that money!

Champa could not understand what he is saying at all. She looked at his face, amazed. When he finished, she said, rather stupidly, 'You want to let out two rooms? How will we manage?'

Suddenly Chitu shook off his diffidence and said firmly, with the authority befitting the head of a family, 'One must manage. How can you say you cannot manage? Perhaps you will not have such luxury, you may even have to do without, what am I to do about this?'

Such luxury! Was Champa really living in such luxury that people felt it was not right? People like Chitu! Was Chitu not here when Champa was living in luxury? When Champa had sat upstairs by the window on a chair, pulled the chintz curtains open and knitted lace, did Chitu never see her at that time? Is that why – he asked her to forsake the 'luxury' of the dump of a room downstairs and 'do without'?

It was but 'doing without'!

Did Champa think of it as a great deprivation when Padmo was made to sleep in the storeroom? Champa too is a single widow, what did she need a whole room for?

When she had dusted off Padmo's clay oven after Mohitosh passed away in order to use it, had Champa imagined even then that she would also have to clean Padmo's old bed and lie down on it? The corrugated tin sheets were very worn and specks of rust rained down on her whenever there was the slightest breeze, mice squeaked on the floors and cockroaches made rasping sounds as they flew at night; sleep was impossible. Did Champa weep?

No, not at all. What did she think of then? Did she try and imagine what Padmo felt like?

After renting the rooms out for a few months Chitu got tradesmen to work on the entire house. There was a new balcony added upstairs. Jyotsna had been dreaming of a balcony for so long. Only the corrugated tin sheets on the two rooms at the back remained unchanged as the money simply ran out when everything else was done. But they were at the back. At the front, the pale pink walls had dark green doors and windows set into them and the red Ranigunge tiles peep over the verandah; all these made the house look like a perfect picture.

One day Champa looked up, amazed at the sight of the new house on her return from a bath in the Ganga as she made her way to the rooms at the back.

Fear

(Bhoy)

Drobomoyi's grandchildren might find it laughable to think that she was once eighteen years old too. But she was once undeniably that age and it was a year marked by tumult in her life.

It was the year that the great earthquake caused the hall built by her grandfather-in-law to collapse and also the same year in which her first born Kartik died. He was a beautiful little child of only three. Just the day before he died he had been fine, sitting on a little red stool as he listened to stories of tigers and crows that stole food from children, as he ate his meal of rice. The next day, he was gone from this earth.

Some said it was caused by a witch. Others said it was an ill-omened wind, a few said it was the effect of an unknown fever. There was much discussion about the cause of death and much was said about what could have been done had it been diagnosed in time. People gave examples of how amulets, incantations and traditional healers had been very successful in treating such cases. Eventually, after satisfying themselves by blaming fate and the machinations of the gods, they stopped talking about the child. The only one who could not be consoled was Drobomoyi.

She thought about all the reasons why Kartik could have died until she grew mad.

No one could make her believe that the little red stool would now be left leaning against the wall of the courtyard forever, never to be used again. She did not weep or cry out loud. All she did was look about stupidly, seeking the child. She became tired with wandering through the huge old house all day long. In the mornings, she would walk out as far as the shed where the cows spent their night with his clothes, his shoes and his little cap, asking whoever she could find, 'Have you seen Katu? Please see if you can find him, he must have wandered off to play with the calf.' As evening fell, she would appear at the door to the kitchen saying anxiously, 'Bamun ma, is the rice not cooked yet? Katu will fall asleep!' At night when Naraan went to bar the door to their bedroom, she would exclaim, 'Why are you locking the door? Katu has fallen asleep in the other room; let your aunt bring him back first.'

Initially, her mother-in-law and the other older women

were full of sympathy but then they began to think that she was overdoing it. In those days, it was rare to find young women who had not felt the pain of losing a child; why else would the mothers whose children had all survived be so valued during all the ceremonies?

But who had ever behaved as unreasonably as Drobomoyi over this?

Her father-in-law and the other elders of the family grew worried and sent for a healer, a Kabiraj; but Drobomoyi could not be made to take the medicines he gave, saying, 'Katu is the one who is sick and you want me to take pills, why, has everyone gone mad?' At first she smiled but then she grew tearful and begged everyone, 'Please tell the Kabiraj to give something for Katu, he has been sick for so many days! I can see him fading away without proper food!'

When the perplexed Naraan put his own heartache aside and became overwhelmed by the need to console his wife and his inability to do so properly in the presence of so many older relatives, Drobomoyi suddenly went and did something that was beyond his worst fears.

Who would have thought that she would go looking for her son on the open terrace when everyone was asleep?

It was amazing that she did not die after falling from the roof to the garden below. All she did was lose consciousness. But the bruises showed up vividly against her fair skin and her hair which had come undone, stuck in a clump to the cut on her forehead making her a frightening sight to behold.

The cut took a month to heal and for some inexplicable reason, Drobomoyi's mind began its journey back to normalcy as her body healed.

Many a winter and many a spring had gone by since that winter. Katu sank into the mists of oblivion in the end. After giving birth to two sons, Drobomoyi gave birth to a baby girl – Shaili.

Shailabala. There can be no other name for a daughter born after three sons. But did she live for long? At the age of four, just after Drobomoyi had her own bangle melted down to make a necklace in the latest style for her daughter and bought Shaili a bright red striped saree to set off her complexion, the girl was unable to fight the pox and passed away.

Drobomoyi did not go mad with grief this time; she only hurt her eyes by weeping continually. By the time she could make up her mind about whether she would put away all her daughter's clothes and toys, give them away to neighbourhood children or hug them to herself each day as she mourned, six months had passed. After that there was no time to think on such matters as she had another new baby – a girl called Sudhalata.

A dark little thing.

But Drobomoyi had lost her taste for beautiful children. All she wanted was for the child to live. She tried to forget the pain of losing the pretty daughter in the company of this plain one.

Fortune is such a thing!

The beautiful babies seemed to come to Drobomoyi only to mock her. Ananda and Gobinda, the two sons who had lived were both quite dark. Yet the baby boy who arrived after Sudhalata's birth with all of Shaili's beauty would not be held for long.

But are all the fruit from a tree equal to each other?

Perhaps the fault lay in Drobomoyi for not looking upon all her children equally.

At the age of thirty two, her sorrow at losing her six-month-old boy grew to such proportions that Naraan had to forget his own pain and tell her off. Even though his words were harsh, the sight of his plump wife thrash about in grief and pray for her own death in a pitiable voice loud enough for everyone to hear from near and far was truly unbearable.

IT was not a result of his words, but gradually Drobomoyi became her old self again. It is said, 'Time is the greatest healer.' Her ambivalence about her surroundings, her annoyance with her husband and her neglect of her three surviving children – all these took about a few months to disappear.

After that, a long period of unbroken prosperity followed.

She gave birth to four more children, who all lived and

staked their claims to the light and air of this world. There was no end of happiness with these children. By the grace of God, they had never known want.

Four sons, three daughters – various rites for them such as rice ceremonies, sacred thread ceremonies and marriages – new sons-in-law, young brides for the sons, leading to grandchildren – Drobomoyi did not have a moment to spare.

It was as if she had stepped on an endless cycle of events that had carried her along for a very long ride.

Upheavals? They had come, of course.

One can hardly expect that a family growing cyclically larger would not shed a few branches here and there? But she was unaffected. The seven children were each well established. Her hoard of happiness grew daily.

She increased her worldly knowledge daily as well.

She was very annoyed when her youngest son's wife, Irabati, stopped doing all housework for a whole week, simply because her brother had died. She was not shy about indirectly referring to this as 'overdoing things' when she talked about it. Why should she be any way? Irabati was always prone to acting up. It would have been something if her brother had been a real person, but he was only three-years-old! Why Drobomoyi herself had lost her parents and a few of her siblings; even the husband who had been her greatest treasure was now dead but she did not give up on the world!

She was in the prime of her life, like the sun shining in the midday sky.

Sudhalata was planning her daughter's marriage; as she had no in-laws, all the responsibility of a senior family member fell on Drobomoyi. Her eldest son Ananda had renovated the old house to build a mansion, the ceremonies surrounding the shift were also entirely her responsibility. Her youngest daughter Padmalata had come to recuperate under her mother's eyes using the excuse of giving birth to not one but two sets of twins; this meant that the children were her mother's responsibility and she did not have to worry about their welfare.

Gobinda, Mukunda, Murari, Snehalata – they all had their claims and their demands on her. She did not have time to breathe. Perhaps she could overlook small losses because she had been given so much.

But Fate does not stop testing us; it pushes us down simply to see how strong we are. One of these challenges happened to Drobomoyi at the age of sixty.

The day before they were to move to the new house, when all the preparations were complete, Ananda died of a heart attack without any prior warning. Drobomoyi was defeated by this most terrible of trials.

Perhaps the family had now forgotten those terrible days but she grew even more terrifying now than during earlier days.

Tremendous sorrow! Maddening in its intensity!

She had not felt a quarter of this when her husband had died; but then of course, she had to stay strong for the children who were all completely dependent on her. But Ananda? Even if she did not admit so, he was her dearest; her most precious.

Was it only the financial support that he provided?

Not at all! It is not enough just to earn money.

Was there such an easy going man of such a casual temperament anywhere else? Who else would be stupid enough to take on the responsibility of four brothers and their families simply because it was his mother's family and not consider that they had duties too? Who else would pay for every kind of comfort for everyone in the family? Who would put up with her innumerable whims?

Where would she now stand for shelter?

BUT removing the shelter from above our heads is a sort of amusement for Fate. Drobomoyi remained while Ananda passed on – the child that had replaced Katu. Why did he have to leave such a bombshell for his mother? Why did he not get to spend a single moment in the house that had occupied his waking hours and his dreams? How would Drobomoyi perform the ceremonies for the house that had been Ananda's dream?

She had not gone easily. It had been very hard to make her break her promise to herself.

She had decided she would not go to the new house. She would much rather become one with the soil that it stood on by giving up food and water. Hers sons, their wives and her daughters all tried to reason with her; they pleaded, argued and shed tears – all to no avail.

She had discovered this easiest of way to bring herself ever closer to death and shed the deep shame of being alive. All of that came to an end when her spiritual guide or Guru came. It was Gobinda's wife who hit upon the idea of bringing him to Calcutta from his home in Santipur.

She had to end her fast at his request.

But she did not enter the new house straight away, choosing instead to go on a pilgrimage. When she returned after seven months, after both mind and body had been restored to health, there was no more objection to crossing the threshold to enter Anand Bhavan.

THAT was twenty years ago.

What happened in the twenty years that lay in between?

She cannot decide where to start when she thinks of those times.

It was hard to make sense of the departures of dear ones. She had barely recovered from having to dress Sudhalata for her final journey with vermilion and wreaths, painting her feet with red aalta when she was called upon to do the same for Snehalata.

There was also that time when she had to go to see Padmalata. Every winter she remembers that journey, the car travelling at lightning speed along desolate streets, her body chilled by the bitter cold, the darkness of that night.

But Padmalata did not have to be dressed in finery, did she? Instead they took her ornaments away from her. In front of her own mother too! No one considered pitying Drobomoyi. Why should they pity her anyway, if she insisted on sitting upright the whole night, her body still unbowed at seventy?

Drobomoyi's heart was so strong, but her sons? Why were they so brittle? Why did they have to fail so often? What need was there for Mukunda to fall into the deepest of sleep while he was sleeping?

SHE cannot remember the years and dates any more. Although she still has the ability to chew sugarcane and extract its sweetness, her memory is not as sharp as before.

Gobinda passed away, too, after being ill for a long time. The only one left, the sole wick left to illuminate Shivratri for her is Murari. His wife never comes to see her; Gobinda's wife shakes her arms, unadorned as befits a widow, before Drobomoyi and gives vent to her bitterness whenever she can, saying, 'Why are you still here? If you went now, at least you would get the fire from your son's hands! But then when I see the state of his health, perhaps not; I say, what gives you the courage to still eat the mix of puffed rice and roasted peas? Truly, your greed has to be seen to be believed!'

Drobomoyi might still be greedy, but is she able to digest all this?

Sickly Gobinda had never earned a good living and she had always been very unpleasant towards his wife; perhaps this was the wife's way of taking revenge for those slights.

Sometimes she lets these things pass while at other times, old habits rear their head and she retorts, 'How dare you say this to me, Shejobouma? Since when have you become so bold?'

'Me, bold? Not at all! I have always been as a servant in this family. But I still need to say what is right. It is only fitting that you go, while at least your youngest son is still alive.'

Fitting!

Drobomoyi stares amazed at her daughter-in-law departing in a huff. Where does this question about what is fitting even come from? Is she still alive because that is her own wish?

Can people do that?

The ones who are gone, did they go of their own will after carefully considering what was befitting? Did her soul not feel torn to pieces as she handed over all that she loved, one after the other to the care of Death? Who will ever understand the torment?

There is no way of making them understand either.

Where is her old ability to fast unto death? These days her heart trembles as the eleventh phase of the waning or waxing moon, the day of the Ekadoshi fast approaches.

Drobomoyi no longer has the strength to wail the names of the ones she has lost.

The only thing left to her are the sensations of hunger and thirst.

Unreasonable tears well up in her eyes when it is time to eat and yet no one brings her food to her. When Gobinda's wife brings a multitude of items set on a stone platter, puts it down before her and says in tones of great disgust, 'Here, get up! A hundred reminders to the kitchen before it is barely ten o'clock. Let me see if anyone else can do all the preparations for cooking and manage to get you your food earlier than this! Like they say, "I will not die, I want to see everything…."' Drobomoyi has to curb her overwhelming desire to throw the plate away not because of the fear of creating a scene or even because of her shame at being admonished, but because of her great hunger.

That is why she sits down hurriedly before the plate and says, a sheepish grin on her face, 'Who went to remind you? Was it Umi, or was it Gauri? Those girls cannot bear to wait! As if their grandmother will fade away if her food comes a few moments late!' She does not admit that she was the one who was sending the girls with the reminders.

'Yes, everyone is just terrified that you will suddenly slip away!' Gobinda's wife answers with a little smile.

Even Drobomoyi does not dare to hope that anyone will soak the ground with their tears at her death, but is there any need to so shamelessly remind her that even the idea of grieving for her is laughable?

Drobomoyi does not have the ability to do much for the household but she does not wish to be removed from it either. But no one will let her do a thing; whenever she tries to do something, her daughters-in-law all express such anguish that it seems she will ruin everything.

'You will hurt yourself! You will hurt yourself!' As if they cannot sleep worrying about her. All pretences! They just do not want her to be a part of the household any more.

She wanders about and ends up in Murari's room.

He does not do anything anymore. The doctor has advised complete rest. He becomes anxious when Drobomoyi sits next to him and his wife Irabati turns her face away and leaves. She must then ask him a few routine questions about his health like a visitor and then leave as well – her request suppressed by fear. She does not tell him about her wish – to be examined by one of the shiny-faced young doctors who come to see Murari all the time. Why does she have a pain in her chest constantly, why do her arms and legs tremble when she stands up, why does the sun's light seem dimmed and the familiar faces blurred in shadows, who else but a doctor can appreciate such fears?

She feels amazed that no one thinks of Drobomoyi when all these doctors visit the house.

Then the day came when the opportunity to raise the subject was lost forever. The doctors needed to visit the house no more.

She lost face before Gobinda's wife. Even the last of her children, Murari was dead. She tried saying it to herself again and again, 'Murari is dead', but it made no sense. But why did her tears dry up like this? Is one not meant to cry over the loss of a son?

TEARS rise for such little reasons, sometimes without reason at all and yet they could not come to her help in an hour when they were so much needed? Truly astonishing.

But her heart ache is worse – can it not be reduced a little? Perhaps, if a good doctor gave her some medicines....

Murari's funeral is held with the right amount of ceremony. It is Irabati's express wish that they celebrate his life; 'He was a great man, we must celebrate that.' 'What can we do if his old mother is still alive?' Is everything to come to a stop just because the old mother seems to have been gifted with eternal life?

Seeing there was so much going on in the house, Drobomoyi could not stay in her room any longer without being involved. She took her cane and wandered around busily, looking for all the world as if she was supervising everything.

No one forbids her today.

Perhaps they do not notice her as they are themselves so busy. Taking advantage of the situation she happily bosses people around a bit, keeping sure they are the ones who have been brought as temporary helpers rather than the old retainers who have ceased listening to her orders for a long time now.

But she suddenly feels confused at the sight of all the people seated to eat. Why are there so many people here? Why are they being fed? Whose marriage is it? No, not a marriage, it is a funeral. But whose funeral is it? Murari's? Who is he? Does she not know him? The world before her flickers like the shadows cast by candle flame and along with all the people, the room and the terrace her cane shakes and her legs seem to be giving way.

Everyone comes running as the cane hits the floor with a sound.

But does anyone feel sympathy? Is she not doing this to punish her family? What was the need to tap around with your stick for show? How do you feel about still showing your face in public? Thank you! Why shouldn't the neighbours feel bad? What a farce!

Even though they did not all feel sympathy they still all came and stood near her. The ones who were eating got up hurriedly. A local doctor, Bhushan Kabiraj, who was waiting to be seated made his way through the crowd. He spoke loudly to ensure that she heard him in her half-conscious state, saying, 'What is the problem? Look at me....'

Drobomoyi looks around uncomprehendingly and says in a strange disjointed way, 'Who is this? Is that you,

Bhushan? Did the proper doctor not come?'

The 'proper' doctors are the ones who came frequently during Murari's illness, the ones who wore proper suits and had stethoscopes hanging from their necks. Bhushan laughed and said, 'What will they do for you?'

'They could check my heart and give me some good medicine.'

A tear or two escaped the corner of her eye.

Her daughters-in-law smirk when they hear what she says and her grandchildren smile.

Bhushan says loudly, 'I will give you good medicine, just tell me, what is wrong with your heart?'

'I don't know, it sometimes feels like it is beating faster, I feel worried, will I get better?'

Bhushan now starts laughing loudly, 'You still want to get better? You are so old.'

Drobomoyi looks at him with her dull eyes, not understanding what he means, 'My age? Yes of course, I am very old. I do not want to live any more... but I am so afraid of dying, so very afraid... Bhushan, why don't you give me some good medicine?'

The Captive Queen

(Bondinee)

A thin mattress about four hands long lies on the floor partially unfolded as it cannot be spread out fully.

Thankfully, the wise Creator has been cutting people down to size ever since time began till they are now three and half spans tall – otherwise there would be no end to the hassles for one human trying to fit his or her arms and legs into a five by four room after all the boxes and broken bits that make up their earthly possessions have been installed.

It is only because people are so much smaller that Charubala has been able to fit her twenty three-year-old son into such a small space filled with so many mismatched things.

The room is stuffy, the pillow torn and the mattress uncovered.

But one cannot blame Charubala for that.

It is not Charubala's responsibility to organise the one thing that is vital if one is to draw a veil over all the ugliness of life.

But how does one sleep so much in this room, on this bed? Shankar wonders why a whole night's unbroken sleep leaves him wanting more.

And yet, one must rise and shine.

He has tutoring at seven and work at nine. During his breaks he must see to the daily needs of the household.

Taranath is of no use whatsoever. It is enough to make one die of shame to think that Taranath is the head of the family but he cannot be trusted with money, however small the amount.

Once he has the money he disappears for the rest of the day.

He returns much later with reddened eyes, reeking of ganja and begins to bully Charubala.

He is not incapable or incapacitated; he is just idle.

Unbearable!

Shankar cannot stand the sight of his father. To him, Taranath feels horribly out of place in the little house with its thin single brick walls on a few square feet of land; like an unnecessary extra in the household.

The mind knows all that goes on....

Shankar cannot help thinking quite often as he looks at Charubala – if the faded borders were completely erased from the edges of her thick, garish, not quite wide enough saree

– how much more worse could it look? Would those two work-roughened, chapped hands look any more graceless if those two cheap gilded brass bangles were taken off?

But he cannot let his imagination get any further.

Taranath may look like your typical emaciated addict but his health is sound.

And that is why Shankar must run around and continue doing household chores, work and tutor with an annoyed expression on his face and hatred poisoning his heart.

He wakes up with the irritating thought that he would have to see his father's face as soon as he stepped outside the room.

Just as he had thought! Taranath was already awake and sitting on the platform in front of the kitchen, smoking a beedi.

His lean muscular face held all the cunning of a fox.

This is Shankar's father.

This is the one who must be revered.

Shankar feels disgusted with himself.

Father and son are barely on talking terms. Sometimes, Taranath does speak to Shankar but his son answers when he feels like it and ignores him when he doesn't.

It is really late. Shankar is quickly splashing water on his face, his shirt slung over one shoulder when Charubala says from the kitchen, 'Don't run off, I am pouring the tea.'

'Let the tea be, I don't have time', Shankar answers as he pulls the shirt over his head hurriedly. Taranath volunteers eagerly without being asked, his words bubbling out with a mouthful of smoke, 'The prince must have his sleep in full and then rush through essentials like bathing and eating!'

Shankar is, however, used to remarks such as this one.

He does not pay any attention at all.

He just flings a disdainful look at his father and continues with what he is doing. But Charubala has already brought the tea.

She holds the cup filled with boiling black tea with her saree and puts it in front of her son, saying, 'If you are already so late you might as well take the money and do the shopping on your way back.'

'Shopping!'

Shankar feels the world crashing around him.

After he comes home from tutoring and shopping for food and has a shower it will be nine o'clock. Even if he discounts the time taken to eat, he will have to consider the time taken commuting.

Commuting!

The distance is not just the four or five miles between the house and work. Commuting means many other things.

Commuting means – a bit of unbearable waiting, being smothered breathless in the embrace of polluted air, a sense of helplessly surrendering yourself to the whims of fate in a kind of unheralded asceticism.

Commuting means – wasting some life force each day.

'If I live, I live', 'If I die, so be it' must be the attitude each day.

Shankar says, somewhat embarrassed, 'Can you not manage today?'

Charubala pleads, 'How can I? There are no potatoes left.'

Which means there is a definite need.

Shopping, going to the ration shop; insurmountable truths of existence, just like birth and death.

Taranath coughs a little to clear his throat and breaks into the conversation between mother and son, saying with a touch of avarice, 'Why bother him if he is already late? Why not give me the shopping bag?'

As if a bag is the only thing needed to go shopping.

There is no need to answer Taranath as he does not expect answers to all the things he says. Shankar is content to smile slightly, contempt and sarcasm evident on his face, but Charubala flares up suddenly.

She screams as if on fire, 'Do you not feel ashamed to say this? Godforsaken, shameless addict!'

Shankar winces on hearing the words.

Who said them? Could it be Charubala?

His ears are filled with a strange buzzing.

THE generally peaceful Charubala is growing uncharacteristically garrulous these days – her language while referring to Taranath is often a shock to Shankar's sensibility, if not as a sign of respect to his father, then surely as a response to his mother's lack of propriety.

But still – such direct and uncouth insults?

He has hated Taranath from childhood but he used to like his mother so much.

When Shankar had not learned yet how to read, Charubala used to teach him to memorise rhymes, poems and stories. When her earrings shook with her laughter as she recited, 'If my baby wants to try, to the flowered forest he may fly', the book lying closed in her hands he truly believed he could do anything he wanted. The perfumes of an unseen flowering forest would fill his childish heart.

In those days, when Charubala wept silently after hearing Taranath's brutal words, he would feel she was like a storybook princess, imprisoned by an ogre; unhappy and helpless.

Growing much bigger to kill the ogre and free his mother used to be all he could dream about.

That dream has evaporated of course, thanks to growing older but he still holds on to that desire to free his mother with the same intensity as before. He wants to keep her in the sort of comfort a princess deserves but he is hopelessly unfortunate.

He had to start working as soon as he finished school, in a very inferior position.

He has had to find tutoring with the little that he knows. What he does for the three or so little boys he teaches is more like shepherding than educating.

Despite this whenever he finds his mother unoccupied he lies down with his head on her lap and spins childishly nonsensical dreams of the comfort he would bring to her life, once he is rich.

As if it is certain that he will be rich.

Mother and son.

One team.

Taranath is alone, an outsider, banned from this world.

But still….

Charubala has slowly been changing for the worse lately.

Her health is gone with lifelong graft, her appearance marked by signs of age.

She spends the whole day without proper clothes on, simply working and continually quarrelling with Taranath.

She seems to be amazed at Taranath's brazen shamelessness every time.

She says, 'A young boy is bleeding away trying to find something to eat – how does a father put that food into his mouth?'

She asks, 'All this time, you at least tried to do whatever you could to support the family, have you become disabled ever since the boy started earning ?'

She says many such things quite pointedly these days but her tone today is extremely vicious.

Shankar was going to say something to change the direction of the conversation. But Charubala seems to grow unusually fierce today. She completely looses her senses and let Taranath have it, 'If a able-bodied man sits around depending on another for all his food, let his mouth be filled with something that is not food at all!'

No matter how much Shankar disrespects his father, he still cannot remain quiet when he hears of the funeral fires being offered to a living man and so he interjects, 'What are you saying Ma!' Charubala seems to erupt instantly.

She says bitterly that she is doing what is totally appropriate! She will say it a thousand times! People who steal their son's earnings to feed their addiction should not just be fed live coals, they should be hanged as well. If he still has a vestige of conscience left in his body, he should go and buy himself a water pot and a hank of rope right now. She will wash the vermilion out of her hair and break her shell bangles to celebrate her widowhood with a sigh of relief.

Taranath is still sitting there smoking nonchalantly, with no outward signs of having heard anything so far but he is roused by the last words she speaks.

He growls at her, 'You are overstepping yourself! You know I forget myself when I get angry!'

Charubala cackles strangely, 'Ooh, you are frightening me! Perhaps I should faint! Watch me do what I promised right in front of you, what can you do?'

And she immediately pulls off the two bangles on her wrists, the ones that had long ceased to tinkle and she starts to rub at the smear of vermilion in the parting of her hair with the end of her saree.

Shankar stares at her in bewilderment.

His senses seem to have frozen.

What is he looking at? The enactment of some tawdry play?

He came to his senses when Charubala suddenly sits down on the ground with the reddened saree pressed to her forehead and a little red leaking from between her fingers.

Taranath might have been patient but even he is not eternally so.

Why should he not pick up a heavy lump of coal lying within arm's reach and throw it at her?

Struck – she suddenly goes completely quiet.

The way in which she sits is so sad and helpless. Was that princess of twenty years ago coming back? Is that why Shankar thinks once again of his childhood wish?

Now he is older; much older; then why not fulfill that wish?

THE dumbfounded Taranath suddenly feels a heavy grip on his neck as he hears an angry roar, 'Get out! Leave right now, not another moment here!'

Why does he forget to be angry? Does he not understand what an insult this is? He stammers an answer; he says, 'Great, young man, great! Say, who are you to drive me out? Do you own this place?'

Shankar gnashes his teeth and says, 'Well, seeing that I am the one paying the rent, I might as well be. I do not want to hear all this, just go get a life.'

Taranath seems even more befuddled and says flippantly, 'Good, good! My life is out there just waiting for me! Where will I stay?'

'Why, you have so many friends to smoke with, one of them will surely invite you in with open arms', Shankar finally leaves the house.

He does not remember why he left the house and wanders about aimlessly for a while before seeing the time on a clockface in a shop and hurriedly getting into a moving tram.

After getting to work, he remembers that he has left Charubala in that state. Perhaps she is still lying on the same spot and the stream of red blood has dried on her cheek. Is Shankar mad? What made him say those things to Taranath, after all he is still his father! He still stays on till the lunch break before asking for some time off. Slavery is such a terrible thing.

If only he could erase the miles between home and work magically.

But as he approaches his house he wonders what is this? What is happening at home? Why are there a couple of boxes and bedding in the front? Why is Charubala tidying the house today, of all days?

Perhaps she is cleaning the room of her unwashed,

hungry son out of compassion? She might not have eaten anything all day either?

Shankar's eyes brim with tears of joy and pity.

He looks for his mother and stops abruptly in front of the kitchen. What is happening there?

Taranath is bundling up some pots and pans with great enthusiasm while Charubala helps, her forehead bandaged with a length of cloth.

'Ma?'

She comes out the kitchen with her hand to her forehead at his call and says calmly, 'It is good that you are here. I was wondering who to give the keys to, as the train is at four o'clock.'

'What train?' Shankar says, his voice almost inaudible.

Charubala answers in the same calm and clear tones, 'The train to the village! Where else? We at least have a few bricks in our own name there!'

Shankar stares helplessly and says, 'Why will you go?'

Charubala speaks in an icy tone that cuts the air, 'I must go dear. It is best I leave before you throw me out as well. When there is no respect for elders, how can I dare to stay here?'

What does Shankar see as he looks at his mother in astonishment?

Can he not recognise the bandaged face? Or perhaps he is trying to understand when it was that all traces of the captive princess were so completely swallowed up by – by that terrifying ogre.

The Mystery That Is Man

(Lok Rahashyo)

Just as the state is vast, so is the machinery that is needed for it to function. In fact, one has to be impressed by all the planning that goes into the functioning of the state.

One such process has started. It is being said that there will be no excuses for not completing this huge task successfully. Thousands of people have been employed to oversee the thousands of others who are involved in the plans behind the planning, supervising the supervisors and ensuring that correct methods are used while following the plans; these people are already half dead with all the work they are having to do.

It is not easy at all.

Forty five million citizens must be bound by the parameters of mathematics and every detail of their lives recorded. Once the life secrets of such a large number of people are known, it will be dissected minutely to yield an infinite number of facts about them. Who goes where, who makes it possible for others to eat daily, how many of them ride in cars, who are the ones who wear saris, what they work at and what their addictions are, who cannot be threatened into saying something sensible and who is so full of sense that it might burst out of them at any time; these details will not be hidden by the darkness of ignorance any more.

But does that mean the job is easy?

This is like taking a group photo of forty five million people.

This photo will help the governments to decide how much of each state is substance and how much is froth and bubbles. This will help them to plan where to put in safeguards and what to ignore.

Does this sound like child's play?

This is not religion that one may make up a few stories to compensate for the lack of actual proof.

In case of the heavens, one may easily transpose fathers and sons and even place an elephant's head on someone who might be missing his own; if there is any confusion over the numbers of limbs due to a mistake in fact-finding we may even stick anything up to ten heads on the same pair of shoulders to make up for the discrepancies and reassure all concerned.

Hence it does not matter whether there are thirty two million deities or forty two million of them as they are easily counted and accounted for.

But this job here is all about humans. Here there can be no inventing of facts.

If you want to cover up your flaws with 'makeup' before a photograph, you will not be able to carry your subterfuge through. A barrage of questions from a hundred clever heads will make you sweat before long.

And any way, why should you conceal your flaws? One must cooperate after all.

I have jumped into the fray with the view of cooperation. I set across this sea each day with a sheaf of forms and a pen for company.

ONE of my many friends asked me quite pointedly, 'For crying out loud! Is this a job for a gentleman? What mare's egg miracle do you hope to achieve by doing this?'

I smiled as I answered, 'If you talk about financial gains to me, I will have to agree they are as improbable as a mare's egg indeed, but the main benefit is the experience I will gain; experience of people and what they are about.'

The friend exclaimed, 'Rubbish!'

'But why do you think this is rubbish? Why, just yesterday, I had quite an experience when I went to a house on What's Its Name road! As soon as I rattled the knocker a gentleman opened the door who could not have been a day below sixty. He was quite stout and fair skinned with a shawl wrapped around him; there was little doubt that he was the owner of the house.'

I asked politely, 'You must be BN Ghosal?'

The reason I said this was that the form had that name listed as the head of the family.

The elderly man frowned and said, 'BN? No sir, I am MN Ghosal.'

My heart was sinking as I thought, 'What! He has a older guardian? A brother surely; his father would be too old to be alive.'

I said meekly, 'Could you fetch your brother for me then?'

'My brother? That will not be possible! I might not even come back if I try to fetch him from the plane where he resides at present. But why are you asking about my brother? What is the matter? Why do you need him?'

'The thing is that this form lists BN Ghosal as the "head of the family".... see here?'

'BN Ghosal? Aha!'

The gentleman smiled detachedly and said, 'What you are saying is that BN Ghosal is listed as the "head of the family"! That is what the prodigal has written then. Very good! Very good!'

I feel smaller than a speck of dust as I see his smile but I still have to persist, 'Look, it says here....'

'Of course, that is what it will say, that is the way he has written it. Well he must have thought it was the right thing to do then, he must think of himself like that but he is my son, Sir. My second son. So he is the "head of the family"? How would you modern types describe it? "The brains of the family"? Ha Ha! How far away do you live? Oh, just locally. You must have seen him then.'

Careful not to smile, I said, 'Perhaps I have, but then I cannot tell as I do not know him!'

'Of course you know him! Try and think. Everyone around here knows him. Why, haven't you seen him walking about, a very well-dressed man, changes his clothes twice a day? Always dressed to the nines from head to toe? He has shoes that match his suits. He carries an expensive folio bag whenever he goes out. He has a certain technique to the way he walks and carries himself. You do not know him? He is my second son, BN Ghosal.'

I concealed my amusement with some effort and said very seriously, 'Should I cross this out and make it MN Ghosal then?'

The gentleman said, 'What can I tell you about your rules! Does one give up the position of family head when one is retired?'

Retired!

Perhaps that is why the second son who is known to everyone decided to remove his father's name from the position. After spending a long time noting down details of all the family members and even the domestic helpers such as their names, family details, education and so on, I asked him at one point, 'Whose dependent should I list you under? Your elder son SN Ghosal or the middle one. BN Ghosal?'

'Must you write me up as a dependent as well? Is that the rule? An elderly father just has to be dependent on his sons, right? You cannot omit that part?'

'Well, with all due respect, you did say you had retired....'

'Yes, I did say that. That is the truth. But I never said that I was dependent on my sons. Take my eldest son for example: Mr SN Ghosal. With my savings I bought him a stationery supplies shop that he has been operating these last three years. Do you think he puts a single coin back towards the family? You have seen yourself the number of children he has, what more can I add as a grandfather? My second son? I think his lordship gets paid about ten thousand rupees a month and spends about twenty. I am the one that has to make up the shortfall. The third son is, however, just the sort I can afford to have. He studies in Jadavpur University. He does not ask for more than what he needs by way of fees, lunch money and bus fares. He manages to pay for his smokes and entertainment out of his lunch money. The youngest is still at school. Now think about it, who am I dependent upon?'

This is the mystery of human nature. Why else would

a man share his pain with a complete stranger like me? But I must complete my work and so I say in my best placatory tones, 'But how do you maintain all these expenses? What is your source of income?'

'My income? These days it is the interest that the bank pays me', the gentleman says despondently. 'And how long do you think I can do that? I am drawing on the principal these days. What was I to do; my son-in-law broke down completely when his daughter's marriage was being finalised! He said it was a loan and that he would pay it back but I am not holding my breath. I know what sons-in-law can be like.'

I could not help my curiosity despite my amusement; I asked, 'All these expenses from the interest the bank pays?'

The man smiled loftily again, 'I know. Remember I told you I worked as an overseer for the government? Just as I was retiring there was a war. Now I hear there may be another one somewhere. Let it be, what is it to a crow when the wood apple ripens? What? Are you done, okay then, Good day to you! You have all that you needed? Please do not say later that your countrymen did not cooperate when you were collecting data.'

THIS was one unusual person. There are more. Do you want to hear another one?

I came to a vast house with gates. It would not be an

exaggeration if I was to say that it was more of a palace. There were flower beds inside the gates. There was a servant or a gardener who sat near the base of a plant with colourful leaves and dug at the soil. I told him to get the owner of the house. He was elderly and somewhat proud as servants in wealthy households tend to be. He asked me without lifting his eyes from his work, 'Which owner?'

'Which one do you think? The master of the house of course!'

'The master?'

The man now dusted his hands off and stood up, saying with a grimace, 'There is not just one master in this house, how will I know who to get without a name of some kind?'

I was dumbfounded. These are not the words of a servant. But what else could he be? He wears an oily faded lungi and an ancient flannel shirt with a woven towel over one shoulder. He has a face covered in salt and pepper bristles.

I understood that he was possibly an old servant with some new gripes.

I opened the form and read from it, 'The name? The name is DP Singh, Retired sub-judge, do you understand? Do get the old master for me.'

The fellow suddenly put his hands into the pockets of his shirt and straightened up a bit, smiled shrewdly and said, 'What need for the old master? Say whatever you must to me. Why, do I not meet with your approval?'

I could have died of shame.

There was no way of running away either, so I mumbled a few words by way of apologising and brought out the forms before explaining the reason why I was there.

DP Singh suddenly started narrating the information, 'So you have come to count people? Good. I have three sons, the eldest is an executive engineer, he is paid twenty two hundred rupees, his name is NP Singh, he is forty two years old; the second one is a doctor and works in Kanpur. I could not tell you how much he gets paid, probably around two and a half thousand rupees, his name is BP Singh and he is thirty eight years old. The youngest is an airplane pilot making eighteen hundred now and hoping for a salary increase soon. His name is SP Singh, he is thirty four and single. Both daughters-in-law are now here. There are twenty seven rooms in the house and two cars. We have twelve servants in total who all get to live here so that they may eat and drink, get haircuts, bathe with soap, watch films and whistle when happy. Sorry, I have left one of them out, there is one other servant who minds the grandchildren and looks after the garden; that is the one who was working here just as you came in. What else do you want to hear?'

I needed to hear a lot more and asked the questions accordingly. But the initial mistake I had made, made my head spin and my words stilted. After answering them all Mr Singh gave me a smile more befitting a fox and said,

'Look now, you did put me down as the head of the family but I hope that my daughters-in-law do not mind if they get to hear of it. It would be better to put the elder one's name there instead.'

Only the gods know how I managed to escape the gates of that house.

DO you want a few more stories? I have many more in stock. I could easily talk about this morning's experience but it will merely make the book heavier.

Now for the story of the father blessed with three daughters.

The gentleman was dealing with the customary twenty questions per member of each household quite smoothly until we came to the topic of the three daughters.

'Their names? I will not tell you!'

I was amazed.

'You won't tell me their names? Why not?'

'Because I feel like it. You cannot force me, that is not the law, I know my rights.'

I knew that too. I still asked politely, 'That is true, we cannot force you to answer any of these questions. But I am just wondering why you are refusing to answer them.'

The gentleman suddenly became quite impatient and said roughly, 'I am not obligated to explain myself. I don't want to tell you, and that is it. Can you do anything about it?'

I was close to losing my cool but I still kept my calm and said, 'No, I cannot do anything about it at all. But then help me with filling in these boxes....'

'Put down Chakravarti's daughters in the boxes!'

'Oh good! Their education?'

'Education? What education? You won't find those overgrown women with their bachelor's degrees and the Master's degrees in this household.'

I was stupefied but the gentleman's words rushed out in a torrent.

'Ordinary Bengali women and education! That is how the Bengali race is going down the drain hole these days! What is education I ask? They know how to cook, they know how to clean, they can wash the clothes and they can even do the dishes if the maid does not turn up! What more do people want!'

I certainly did not want much more and I was able to fill the form up but for one small detail. Their ages; this was essential.

I asked with polite hesitation; that scion of the ancient sages Mr Chakravarti immediately summoned all the fierce indignation of his ancestors and turned his blazing eyes upon me like electric beams.

'Age? Whose age?'

'Your daughters', who else?'

'My daughters'? Really? Have I not already told you that they are unmarried?'

My eyes wide with astonishment, I persist, 'Yes, you did say that.'

'Then what more do you want? Why do you want to know how old these unmarried girls are? What kind of a fellow are you? Just because you are doing a government job does not mean you can take liberties! How old are they – what next!'

Whether a government job entitles me to take liberties or not, it has definitely taught me to block my ears to insults and shield my back from blows; and so I ask again, 'You might not want to share their names, but their ages too? Tell me quickly.'

'Quickly? Really? Fine, I am putting my foot down. Let me see how you extract anything out of me! I will not tell you how old they are! You are asking for the names of decent Bengali girls, you are asking for their age! Then you will spread all this all over the place and the little chance that they have….'

I could not be angry with him after hearing this. I smiled and said, 'You are mistaken; none of this will be made public.'

He laughed a bitterly dismissive laugh.

'Governments and in confidence? I know all about that sir! I have seen a lot in my fifty three years, and I read all the top secret government stuff in the daily papers.'

'Fine, I agree with all that but what of these empty boxes?'

'You will not let it be, I can see! Just write down – they are over sixteen!'

'All three?'

'Yes, all three! At least that way, I am not making anything up!'

I do that and escape from the house with great relief.

But have I escaped?

Not really, as I see Mr Chakravarti bearing down on me.

'Listen please....'

He is wearing a formal coat. He clasps my hands and says pitiably, 'Are you going away in anger?'

I extricate my hands and say, 'Why would I be angry?'

'I gave you enough reason. Please do not mind, I am upset over various things. Listen, I will tell you their names but not their ages. You understand do you not? Saying they are over sixteen does not mean that they turned sixteen the other day, does it? They turned sixteen years ago. Therefore, I will tell you their names and even show them to you. Why do you not come back in and see them?'

What does he mean by see them!

I manage to say with great difficulty, 'Who will I see?'

'Why, my three daughters. You are like a son to me; I will use the familiar *tumi* with you from now. You are going from door to door and seeing so many people, find me three grooms.'

'What are you saying? Grooms for your daughters?'

'Why, nothing wrong in that! You know all the details of the young people. You are a Brahmin yourself and unmarried, are you not?'

I am amazed, 'How do you know that?'

Mr Chakravarti cackles knowingly and says, 'I can tell all that from just looking at you. Why do you not come in and take a look – just as they are. There is no soaps and powders stuff in this house. You will see for yourself – they are not hideous.'

Apparently he was certain that I was going to go back and see the girls.

I smiled and said, 'But what you need is three men. I alone can hardly….'

He said regretfully, 'I know! It is not even like the old days when one could give three daughters to the one man. Well, why do you not select one? Then you can take the responsibility for your sisters-in-law! Ha Ha!'

He obviously felt that this was humour of the highest order and continued to chuckle in a self-satisfied manner.

'Not now, I am busy….' I say and make my escape.

That was some days ago.

I have not been back there since that day. I am scared to be around a man who can tell my caste group from looking at my face and correctly picks whether I am married or not.

You want any more examples of how strange people can be?

You will have to wait for me to collate more data. I am

still going to knock on doors and ask about the 'head of the family' for two more weeks. Even more complicated individuals are bound to turn up.

I am sure they will turn up. Who was it that said, 'How unusual is this land!' Was it Seleucus or DL Ray? Who said those words?

I do not quite remember but the tune is still fresh in my mind.

A Terrible Tale

(Ekti Korun Kahini)

I went to Darjeeling during the holidays where we stayed at the Louis Jubilee Sanatorium.

An eagle eye for both the pleasures of travelling and tradition has made me take refuge in the orthodox guesthouse where there are a few ladies in the adjoining rooms who are similar to me.

We even became quite close to one of the families after going to view the sunrise from Tiger Hill with them one day.

But I have carefully hidden the little fame that I have garnered for myself in the outer world from these new friends.

They are in Room 11 and we are in Room 13. The woman with the family in the room between the two is very young and she has been assiduously avoiding the gray-haired crowd. This has meant avoiding the room next door and going to the room on the other side when in need of conversation.

Room 11 frequently visits our room and seeing the scattering of the festive literary magazines or Pujabarshikis on our table (the gentleman living with me in Room 13 brought a stack of them with him, having had a wish to read them all during the holidays), observes happily, 'I see you have the same habit of buying books as I do! How much money have you wasted buying all these? I also spend a lot of money during this period to feed the habit, but it is nothing like yours.'

I do not give any indication that these were all writer's copies presented to me and that I did not have to waste any money for them at all.

I give an all-knowing and loaded smile in answer. But I do not express my agreement with the fact that it has been a waste of money in her case.

Number 11 says, 'You cannot tell because I am so busy with all of you here, but I spend every hour of my day with books. I get scolded so many times by my husband. But what can I say, I just cannot! I just cannot bear to be parted from a book for a moment.'

Things were going splendidly.

Then there was an amusing incident.

It was nothing major. It was just one of those things that happen.

What is an incident? I have looked for incidents in all the things that have happened in my life but none of them can be called an incident. The muse of incidents bad and good has never looked upon me with favour.

Things that happen in everyone's lives are hardly worth mentioning when they happen in your own.

When a dog bites a human being, it is hardly news now is it? It is only newsworthy when a human being bites a dog.

It is truly a matter for great regret that I cannot find one incident in my entire life that I can build a 'true story' around.

But I have noticed that everyone else seems to have events packed into their lives. Some seem to gather incidents like crops.

You will see proof of that in their life stories and in their travelogues. If they go on a trip, events begin dogging them right from when they board the train. The young and the beautiful who seem populate every hotel, temple and restaurant these lucky people go to will inevitably fall in love with them. Events happen and lead to more events in turn.

How much easier it is for them to write 'true stories'.

There is real artistry in knowing how much impurity must be mixed into gold to keep it pure and how many tales to blend into truth to make it a 'true story'. Not everyone can master that art form.

Any how – what was it that I was going to say…?

ONE day the bellboy in the hotel mixed up our mail and took our letters to Room 11. We had been getting letters carrying the season's greetings ever since the festive season ended.

I saw that the lady from Number 11 was coming our way in a hurry with two letters in her hand. She held them out to me and asked, 'Is this yours?'

I took it and turned them over to find an envelope and a postcard. They were from my daughter and my sister. I smiled politely and said, 'Yes they are mine. Did he drop them off along with your mail?'

'Yes, what a mess! What a fool, why did he give us letters meant for Room 13?'

Even though it was not such a great mistake on the part of the local fellow who was the bellboy, I still said, 'You had to come all this way because of his mistake!'

'What of that? It is nothing. Actually, I feel much better that he did make the mistake.'

Better because of a mistake?

'Now I have found you out! You thought you would be able to hoodwink me, but see now? Now tell me, why did you not tell me who you were in all these days of talking to each other?'

I smiled, 'Who I was?'

'No, no more hiding! Thank God! the mail got mixed up. I hope you do not mind, I read the postcard sent by your sister. That was how I found out.'

I had read my sister's postcard by then too. I noticed she had asked me whether I had found my next story among the quiet lanes bordering Calcutta Road in Darjeeling.

Number 11 said again, 'What a thing to do! Such a great person living right next door and you never said a thing!'

'A great person! Please!'

'You are too modest. Who has not heard of you in Bengal? I truly do love your stories so much!'

I smiled in a suitable way at this.

In fact, I suddenly began to think of her as being quite sensible after all.

This was the first part of the incident.

Then I found her dragging her poor husband to come and see the writer next door. I had heard that he was a businessman who probably spent all his time watching prices rising and falling at work. What a situation to find himself in!

I smiled and said, 'We meet daily.'

Number 11 smiled and said, 'That is different, this is seeing a new persona.'

Imagine my luck! Unveiling a new persona and in front of such an unappreciative audience. But less of that, what if this story falls in the wrong hands.

But I will still have to admit that the gentleman was good natured.

When I spoke to him it became clear that besides knowing that writers wrote, he had never devoted a second thought to their tribe but he still submitted to a literary discussion with a real live female practitioner simply at the whim of his book-obsessed better half.

The discussion flowed along these lines: how much did I make each month from writing on average? Why I did not self- publish but gave it to a publisher? What proof did I have that my publisher was honest with me? What kind of contract, if any, did I sign? Was there any relationship between an editor and a publisher? Why did film makers not buy their stories in bulk from the book shops instead of paying so much more to the writers? And so on and so forth.

The evening passed. The next morning I found that Room 11 was so proud of her discovery that she was waiting at the door with a smile and three or four other women.

The small room was filled with things and I could not decide on how to seat them all. I chased my husband out to the lawn. The ladies who had come along, each seemed equally overwhelmed and said, 'Not in my wildest dreams did I imagine that I would ever meet you like this! I love your work! Tell us, how do you do this whole writing thing? When did you first learn to write?'

They said many more things but if I write all that down

you may think that I am trying to blow my own trumpet. Suffice it to say that this became a common occurrence every day. The devotees came whenever they felt like it.

Number 11 said with a beaming face, 'Remember, how you hid away! How can you hide a fire like yours under a bushel?'

The comparisons filled me with joy. My confidence in Number 11's powers of judgment grew daily. These days I do not cringe in disappointment when I see her coming, I invite her in with the greatest hospitality.

I do not send my husband away these days either. I tell him to stay under the quilts and not risk catching a cold outdoors.

She always comes after an afternoon trip. She always opens with a discussion of how much she reads all the time. She is not satisfied with being a member of only one library and has to have books from no less than two lending rooms, some nights she sees the dawn in as she forgets to sleep and she was frequently in trouble with her mother-in-law for reading so much – these are stories that I am learning by rote. Of course, she praises me too when she takes a break from narrating her own stories.

'All my life I only read and read, never learning to write one bit. I feel jealous when I see you. Really, how well you write! When I was reading "Eclipse" by you, I cried so much I thought I would never stop. It was not enough to read it on my own, I had to read it aloud to my husband too.'

This goes on till the ringing of the dinner bell.

The man in Room 13 pokes his head outside the quilt and sighs deeply, once she leaves. 'Alas!'

'What are you sorry about?'

'Room 11's husband. I feel like weeping for him.'

TIME passed in these pleasantries till it was nearly the end of the holiday. We were leaving the next day.

I was frantically packing our things much in the manner of the ancient caravans when Room 11 appeared at the curtain to the door. With her was a young woman.

It was not someone new but the lady from Room 12. I guessed that she had not come to meet the brilliant writer in Room 13 earlier because she did not mix with most of the people in the hotel. She was probably ruing the fact now.

Number 11 looked at my method of packing suitcases and said, 'So you are leaving then?'

I smiled and said, 'We all have to leave at some point.'

'That is true.' She sighed and smiled at the same time, a little like a philosopher.

'This hotel was like a microcosm of the earth. People come and go, their stays are pre-destined. They become close friends only to part company at the end. This is so like the world.'

I was pleased at this expression of her way of thinking.

Once I had such a different opinion of her. How quick we are to judge people.

She continued, 'How pleasant it was to be living together for these past few days. I will remember this forever. I will talk to everyone about it.'

Number 12 was standing there with an unpleasant calculating look on her face.

I know that some people affect this look.

'I judge all of you and find you to be lacking', this is the attitude that some people seek to display in their behavior.

It is hard to be hospitable before this attitude but she was still a guest.

The solution was provided by Number 11.

She looked at Number 12 with a peculiar mix of reproof and humorous censure, saying, 'Why are you quiet? This is the right place to clear up all your doubts.'

I smiled and asked, 'What doubts?'

'What can I say? She has been arguing with me all this time. She does not think you are a writer at all, you have only successfully pretended to be one because I am not that clever. Apparently she knows the person you are pretending to be. Can you imagine? You are so modest and she thinks you are an imposter!'

I do not know what my face looked like at the moment but I suspect it was a look of pure bewilderment.

Before I could speak, Number 11 spoke in an amused tone, 'Next thing I know, you will be saying you have lived in Bhagalpur all your life and never seen this woman there.'

'Go on – say what you said before – that you have seen many imposters like this; that you have seen her name entered in the hotel's register as Gupta! Everyone will laugh at you! Apparently your husband's surname is Gupta!'

I had finally found my voice again. I said with a somber smile, 'She is right, our surname is Gupta.'

Number 11 spluttered, 'What a thing to say! You are called Mrs Singh and he is Mr Gupta?'

'Why would I be Mrs Singh?'

The woman became a little crestfallen at my words.

She asked me glumly, 'Why, are you not Ashalata Singh?'

'No!'

The young woman smirked and turned on her heel smartly on her way out of the room.

But Number 11 still stood there. I felt a little sorry for her when I saw her face. I said to her with a smile, 'What name did you see written on the letter the other day? Try and think....'

'I don't know, I just looked at the name, did not realise whether it said Singh or Gupta. Your sister had mentioned something about a story and so I assumed you were a writer. This is one of my faults, I never have the patience to read things till the end. Any way, you have had much amusement at my expense for the last few days! Number 12 is clever and did not fall for your tricks,'

I could not say what was on the tip of my tongue. There was no point mentioning how she had cried when she read 'Eclipse'. Besides, who was it that had to provide amusement to her and her friends?

An Act
(Obhinetri)

A place has been set in the middle of the courtyard where an impossibly big plate sits surrounded by eight or more bowls. The arrangement is old fashioned and seating has been made on the floor with a carpet square for warmth and comfort. All of this is meant not for a new son-in-law but rather for a new father-in-law.

The relationship is young and the daughter-in-law's father has come from far away.

The lady of the house is said to be very shy and thus the responsibility of overseeing the hospitality has been handed to the daughter-in-law herself. The decision was not wrong at all. Even though the daughter-in-law is young she seems to have the determination needed to be able to make one person eat the equivalent of three meals.

In a husband's house, one's father and brothers are all guests; why shouldn't Anupama entreat her father to eat just a little more?

Her father smiles and says, 'I see you have become a real mistress of the house! Special treatment as guest for me too? Have I ever eaten this much?'

Does Anupama not know that he does not eat this much? But the rule is to implore. Besides, even though her mother-in-law will not be present herself, she will be watching from behind the scenes and point out Anupama's failings later. Anupama starts again with enthusiasm, 'Well… if you will not eat all the fish, you will eat the sweet dishes? This sweet cheese is from our country home Father, you must not leave the table without eating these!'

'Then you sit down and eat them!' Her father smiles and stands up. He does not give his usual lecture on 'wasting things'.

The incident happened two years ago. Cutting corners on hospitality for fear of waste was frowned upon in those days. Inviting a person to eat and then serving him just enough food for one was unheard of. What was the point of hospitality if there wasn't any waste? It was a sign of emotional poverty if people placed food above a guest.

Even in their wildest nightmares had people never thought that a day would come when food would be rationed. Anupama rose with her father and did not worry in the slightest about whether a crow or a stray cat decided to fly off with a leftover from his plate. As she walked by his side, she said in a barely heard voice, 'You will ask to take me with you?'

She had not been able to say anything all this while as there were eyes and ears watching them during the meal.

Her father answered her in the same tone of voice, 'That is why I came. If I return alone this time, your mother may not spare my life. I am thinking we could take the train tomorrow morning.'

Anupama's young heart trembled in anticipation, anxiety and apprehension, she could not bear to be here for another moment. 'Tomorrow morning' seemed so far away.

But she was a daughter-in-law. The times were different. It was completely wrong to even express a wish to visit one's parents. And so she whispered like an old matron to her father, advising him, 'Make sure you say things properly father, you know how my father-in-law is a little irritable?'

'A little?' Her father almost laughs out aloud, 'Say that he is very irritable! It is hard to stay calm in the face of all his snide remarks. Anyhow, this time I am going to try everything....'

A little reassured, Anupama winks at her father to silence him. She has heard footsteps and she does not want to risk being taunted about asking her father to take her home.

Her mother-in-law might be shy but she is not shy about showing her impatience with Anupama.

AN hour later, the scene is repeated in the courtyard with the master of the household. He is seated on a less plush square of matting and four or five bowls surround the plate he is eating from. Anupama sits at a side with a palm leaf fan.

Even though he is no guest, she still implores him to try and finish everything as she would a guest. This too is the rule. Everyone wants their son's wife to take care of them.

Anupama knows how to fulfill these wishes.

After eating for quite a while, the master seems to suddenly remember something and looks up. He says, 'There was something else… your father has been asking if he can take you home with him.'

'Let him say what he wants', the fan moves faster. She wants to hide the thudding of her heartbeat.

'How can I let him be?' her father-in-law says sarcastically. 'He is determined this time. Apparently if he does not go back with you, your mother may refuse to let him into the house.'

'She is the real problem!' Anupama heaps sugar into his bowl of yogurt and says dismissively, 'She has such strange whims! Tears every time she wants to see her daughters. What is this? My poor father – that one time, my elder sister was supposed to come during the festive season and she couldn't – my mother stopped eating for a week. Everyone was dressing up for the festival except for my mother! Now tell me, is it always possible for people to do as they say? They have their own families to look after!'

There is a slight flicker of amusement on her father-in-law's face as the somber mask lifts. 'Well, I have agreed to send you with your father', and he pulls the bowl of sweet rice pudding closer.

Anupama's face lights up as well. But she disguises it with a false look of sorrow, puts the fan down and puts her hand to her mouth in surprise, 'What? Why did you do that? Mother has been unwell and our sister arrives in two days. The cook has been saying he will "go home!"' Anupama seems to visibly wilt with worry.

'Well, there is no point.' The master squeezes two lemons into his glass of water and savours his drink while his words seem to hang in the air.

Anupama's mother might be obstinate but Anupama cannot afford to behave like that. As she puts away the salt and the sugar she says wisely, 'What will our sister think if I go away to my parents' now? Tell my father that it cannot be.'

'That won't be possible', the master stands up slowly, balancing himself on his left hand as he rises, 'the word of a man is like the tusk of an elephant. Once I have said yes, I am not going to renege on my word.'

What can Anupama say after that?

It takes a lot of time to subdue the jubilation on her face and so she takes her time with her father-in-law's shoes, towel and other things. She then says, 'This could be a problem. Why does he need to take me at this time? While Mother is unwell and all….'

This 'Mother' is her mother-in-law.

Not even her biggest enemy would say that the plump woman shows any signs of illness, but Anupama sees every sign of ill health. This is one way of keeping both parents-in-law in good humour.

THE next part of the story takes place not in the courtyard but in a room and not at day but at night.

She is tearfully describing to Taranath how much she will miss him.

What can Anupama do if the two fathers decide on sending her away? She did not want to go at all at this time. At least if there was a reason for the trip. But her mother is so very obstinate. But Anupama cannot say all this. So she has to use all the ruses she knows to express her sadness at leaving him so that he is appeased.

There is a fourth scene to this. It takes place against the background of Anupama's parental home. But we will not talk about it here. Let us talk about the present instead.

THE place is the same. The people are the same too. The same courtyard, the same Anupama, fan in hand. Her face is slightly changed, her complexion is not as bright but her hair hides the grey well.

In front of her sits Taranath, the present head of the family. He is unchanged as well, except for the weight of twenty five years on top of the original twenty five.

The seating and the utensils might be from his father's times, but the food is stamped with the austerity of today. Housewives of today no longer implore people to eat a little more. Instead each day, Anupama expresses wonder at things that were as cheap as water in the old days and how prices have risen sky-high at present. She also declares that it will not be possible to live so lavishly for much longer.

Their son struts about like some royal scion. Their daughter seems to think she is of royal blood. The slightest error and they create havoc. Anupama never says this within their hearing though, one can never tell with young people these days.

There will be no discussing prices today for the master is angry. Anupama holds her tongue.

After a little while Taranath asks, 'What was the young Lord arguing about earlier?'

The 'Lord' in question is their unemployed son. Who else can be the focus of such acerbic comments but one's grown up son?

Anupama makes a sound to express her annoyance and says, 'What can I say? Now it is all about going to Delhi! His friends are all going, so he must as well! He is all riled up over going to Delhi.'

Taranath says angrily, 'Is he still persisting with that whim? I am telling you for the last time… there will be no going to Delhi!'

'I told him the same thing, but would he listen!' Anupama says, putting the fan down and gesturing with her hands. 'He keeps saying, "Why should I not go?"… "What is the harm in going?"…"Don't people go to Delhi?"…"Are people dying because they went to Delhi?"… "There has to be a valid reason for saying no to everything!" and all this sort of big talk!'

There has to be a valid reason for saying no to everything!

Just listen to his audacity! His father's unwillingness should be reason enough. He needs more reasons? Angrier, Taranath says, 'I am not his employee that I must give him a reason. I am not going to let him go to Delhi with a bunch of good for nothings! I am the one to pay for all this! At least I would understand if he had the ability to earn his own keep. He has to stick his hand out in front of this old fellow even for the money for a haircut and still so much pride! He cannot even talk to me properly! Am I not worth his time?'

Anupama continues in the same vein; 'It is not just you! They do not give anything in the world its dues, and that thing you said about putting his hand out for money! I would be happy if he did that but no, he has too much pride! I have to ask him again and again whether he needs anything... as if he does me a favour by accepting!'

'Hmm. You have the same useless pride but still I must say this, you are the one responsible for his nature', Taranath observes.

'When did I spoil him?' Anupama is not pleased. 'You do not know what a temper he has! Do you think I can say a lot to him?'

'I am sure I would have said a lot more than you ever did, I would have! If I did not have to worry about you!' Taranath says.

Suddenly a mysterious smile plays across the middle aged Anupama's face, one more suited to the age of twenty four than her forty something years. Her answer, however, befits her. 'What a thing to say! As if you are constantly in fear of me. If there is anything to fear, it has to be the young people these days. Our son was saying the other day that some friend of his had an argument with his father and... who goes there? Who is that?'

Taranath says, 'Who else will it be? Must be the servant Medho!'

'Who knows', Anupama is perplexed, 'Seemed like the boy walked upstairs.'

'Where would he come from? I just saw him leave, all dressed up and everything. He never goes anywhere without a portfolio dangling from his hands, like some sort of big shot!'

'Yes, he does do that. But, I hope he did not come back?'

'Why, what would he come back for?'

'Who knows, perhaps he forgot something. The other day he came back, going a long way. Apparently he had forgotten his watch!'

'Of course, he would do that! The world would fall to pieces if he did not have his watch strapped to his wrist! Why, ask him to run and get something from the shops? Then he acts like the sky has fallen on his head!'

After saying these things with some annoyance, Taranath takes a little lemon quarter and squeezes it into a glass of water. The price of lemons these days means that one can no longer afford two whole lemons per glass.

Before responding like a faithful wife to this latest sharp remark from her husband, Anupama gets up and looks this way and that from the door before she can be certain that there is no one out there. She then proceeds to give examples of all the youth of today who have studied all the books but never manage to smarten up or behave better. She has seen her nephews, Taranath's nephews, and everyone in between. She is not the sort of stupid mother who is blinded by love to her son's faults. What is the use of passing three sets of exams if all he has done since then is chat with his friends and watch films for two years? Why, could he not have looked hard and found something in the time? At least it would have helped his father.

She says much of great value and import. Taranath is not in a hurry to go anywhere, there is no work today.

Eventually he gets up, chews some mouth freshening paan and goes to the living room where a neighbour comes to play chess with him each weekend.

ANUPAMA had only just sat down to her meal after all the servants had eaten when her daughter Sheila appeared and said hurriedly, 'Cook, is the range still on? Can you boil some water for tea quickly?'

Water for tea! At half past one in the afternoon!

Amazed, Anupama says, 'You want tea now?'

Sheila says with some irritation, 'Not me! My brother has a terrible headache.'

'Your brother? Is the boy at home?' Anupama's blood freezes at the thought.

'Of course he is. He went out and came back because his head was hurting. Cook, did you make the tea?'

In Sheila's world, the only person who is worthy of respect is her brother.

Anupama manages to swallow her food as fast as she can and rushes upstairs to her son's room where she sits down on the bed. Fearfully she asks, 'What is wrong my son? You went out and then came back with a headache? Are you ill?'

Naturally there is no response to these expressions of motherly affection and concern.

As soon as she tries to touch his body and feel for a fever her hand is pushed away and her son turns on to his side.

Anupama pays little attention to this rebuke and asks again, 'When did you come back?'

Silence.

She is now certain that he has heard every word of the high-level discussions between his parents. But she did not come here to return defeated, so she says with genuine feeling, 'you are feeling ill today? Do you not have to leave for Delhi the day after tomorrow?'

Leave? Judging from the way in which her son frowns at her, he hardly seems like a child any more.

'Leave? Where am I going?'

Anupama acts simple, uncomprehending even, like a child, asking in all innocence, 'Why, you did say you were leaving on Tuesday?'

'They are leaving, how does that matter to me? They have their own money, they can do as they please!'

Suddenly Anupama squeals in laughter, almost like Sheila. She uses the same tone of voice she once did twenty years ago to bring her obstinate son under control and says, 'Aha! So the boy is angry? Who has scolded you? Who dares slap you? Who has used harsh words? I suppose you overheard your father's sharp words? (She leaves her own remarks out without a single qualm. Not a sign of guilt clouds her expression.) I was wondering what was wrong with my boy today! Look, I told you I would get you the money!'

'Where are you going to get it from, it will not simply fall from the skies? It will still be Taranath Ray's money, will it not? I don't want to go on holiday like this, let me sleep for a while. The unemployed are not meant to have these dreams.'

Anupama dismisses her son's words saying, 'Yes, sure! You are too old to ever find a job now aren't you? Slapping labels like 'unemployed' on yourself? Who cares about what he says? Has he ever made any sense? If we were to listen to him, no one would eat well or wear good clothes, visit relatives or anything! We would all be counting money all day long!'

'Perhaps that is what I should do! At least as long as I am living under his roof', her son says bitterly.

'Yes, sure! I have been living at his mercy all my life, am I not? It is only by saying the right things and keeping him pleased. What is the point in being obstinate and failing to get ahead? Your grandfather, now he was worse with his terrible rages! If he said "No" once, that was it! I was the only one who could flatter him and cajole him….'

This time her son says angrily, 'Why did you? You did wrong! Why must you flatter someone? You have done the same with our father. But why? Do you not have an identity of your own? Do you not know right from wrong? Can you not see reason on your own?'

A subtle smile plays on her face, just at the corner of her lips.

Reasoning? Does she not know how to reason? She has so much that if she opens the floodgates, both father and son would be washed away by her reasoning. But how does Anupama manage without them? Reasoning? If she had ever tried to display that, she would have not been around to see all this.

And identity?

Even that has been blended, watered down, dried and put away neatly. If he dislikes flattery and cajoling so much, what does her son think she has been doing with him for the past few minutes?

But she says nothing about all this and the subtle smile fades away. She only says dejectedly, 'What will you know of why I do not have an identity? Is everything clear just because you read more books? Do not hurt me anymore, I will not be able to bear it if you have to stay here while your friends all go to Delhi. Let him be angry with me. I have never gone anywhere nor seen a thing and have stayed locked away all my life. If you people get to see something on holiday, my heart feels rewarded.'

Her son looks at her, embarrassed. It seems to him that her eyes hold the weight of all her disappointments. The burden of her life, unfulfilled, captive and helpless as it was.

Then the discussion changes tack. Sheila joins in, tea in hand. They discuss all the places Anupama will go to once her son can pay for it. Some times, they cannot agree and Anupama tries to convince him, 'If we are to go after all this time, then why go to Mussoorie? Let us go to Puri or Bhubaneswar instead.' Sheila is a great fan of her brother and so she makes fun of her mother's choices. But her brother changes his mind too for those are examples of Indian sculpture, and his mother's choices are not to be sneezed at.

Then they talk about the things they would buy. A 'Katki' saree for Sheila and brass utensils for their mother; even the next trip they will take is discussed.

Three hours have passed. It is now half past four. Suddenly there is a tremendous exclamation outside.

'Is there not any tea today?'

Startled, Anupama looks at the clock, 'Four forty! Disaster!' Taranath has his 'teatime' at exactly four o'clock. If he does not get his tea at that time, his heart starts to trouble him.

Whatever the state of her own heart at this sudden verbal assault, Anupama keeps her expression composed and says with genuine regret, 'Oh no! Is it that late? Look at us! Sheila, why did you not say a thing? The servant must be sleeping his head off as well!'

'True, I can expect a paid servant to see to my comforts with a lot more care.' Taranath observes with as much vitriol as he can pour into his words.

What does Anupama feel like saying when she hears him?

A retort about 'an unpaid maid perhaps?'

Who knows? She does not say anything so no one knows. She only brings a tone of natural concern to her voice and says, 'See, our son has taken to his bed because he is not feeling well. I wonder if he is coming down with a fever? With all that is happening!'

THE next scene takes place not at day but in the night.

It is no longer in this room but in another one. After locking the door, Anupama hands two tablets of Ptycho soda and a glass of water to her husband and sits on the bed with her own box of betel leaves. She opens the container with its many compartments filled with ingredients to prepare paan and takes a pinch before saying, 'Your heart is not troubling you too much, I hope? You become so unwell when your routine is disrupted – oh, we are not talking now? You will not look at me? You are angry, are you? Really, you are impossible! You are like a child with all your anger! And your son is just like you… whether he has learned anything else from you, he has certainly inherited this temper! Remember how I said he was ill? Turns out he was not ill at all, simply angry! All his friends had finished packing and he was fuming over that. So I got angry with him and told him to go. What if he made himself unwell with all this anger? When Sudhir and Shyamal are going, let him go as well. Let us see whether he grows an extra limb after going to Delhi! If he can find a job on this trip, it would prove he has some brains at least. Doesn't Shyamal's uncle work in a high post over there? Tell me, hasn't your friend Subodhbabu also been transferred to Delhi recently?'

'He has, but he is hardly going to get a job for your son as soon as they see each other', Taranath says with a cynical smile.

'You are incorrigible!' Anupama smiles, just as she did ten or twenty years ago. She leans back on the pillow and says, 'You tease me all the time! Now move a little and let me lie down. Oh no, I was going to put the mosquito net up… wait a little while I do that.'

'Let it be!' Taranath places his hand on her head and says, 'You don't have to pretend that you are going to do that. Why this sudden awakening of a sense of responsibility?'

'No, you are not well today', Anupama replies, sitting up hurriedly. But Taranath is already on his feet. He smiles through his moustache and says, 'Such a faithful wife! How many times would you say you have done this in the past twenty seven years?'

The dyspeptic Taranath does not fall asleep quickly while Anupama drops off immediately exhausted by her long day and by the strain of maintaining her pretences. Perhaps sleep comes quickly because of the relief that comes from such perfect acting.

Acting?

What else is it? Perfect flawless acting. So flawless that it is hard to see that she is acting. It is impossible to see which of the things she does are real and what is manufactured.

But it is not just Anupama. Are all women not actresses? Being able to pretend is the capital they work with. Everything they do through their lives is funded by this capital.

She who has more of this capital is more successful in life, with more fame, name and praise showered on her.

She can hardly afford to flow free as a river. She cannot afford the stupidity of losing one bank at the expense of building up another. She must keep both sides happy. She must keep her family happy because that is where she can find her own feet.

The thing she fears most is the lack of love, the cruelty of neglect.

Or is this all wrong on my part?

None of this is pretence. A woman has always been home to two separate identities… the mother and the lover. She is completely fulfilled in both of those.

Women provide shelter to the ignorance and childishness of men… like two great wings to shield men with care and tenderness.

This is not pretence but compassion. If this compassion did not exist, how long would men last before the cold clarity of the world? How long would it take for them to be ruined?

Refugees

(Udbastu)

'You must agree to this from a humanitarian angle Dibu! If we do not look after our own then what chance....'

Raju seems pleased at being able to use such big words; at least that is what the self-satisfied look on his face indicates; as if he has managed to convince me with his reasoning.

But I have other problems. I cannot just look at the humanitarian angle and not think of the human being I have been living with for the past ten years, the one who has been instrumental in the success of my human existence. Even though I agree to taking on a tenant, she has firmly put her foot down.

She will not have tenants. She says, 'What house for rent?

Say you have a room for rent instead! Of course, if you had a couple of houses around the place, we would rent them out. But renting out half of the place we are living in? Shame on you for even thinking that would be possible!'

It is true though, I did propose letting out half of the house we live in for purely financial reasons. We can live very comfortably on one floor with our only child and let someone else live downstairs. We are not wealthy, we do not have a couple of spare houses but we do have a large house to ourselves. If we can get a clerk's salary worth of rent money from the part that is not used, who would say no?

I know it is not very pleasant to think of letting your house out to other people but if we can ignore the niceties and get a tenant in, the monthly reward that will follow? Is there any sound sweeter than the jingle of coins?

But what can I do?

I cannot do anything with the house if the housewife is not agreeable. And so – in this current climate of golden opportunities, in this season of netting the big one – I must merely look on and listen to stories of people getting a hundred and fifty rupees for one and half rooms and others getting so much money for a temporary structure raised next to their balcony that they could have built a balcony each month with the money before the war broke out.

I do not try to convince her a second time. No point in angering her. She will still say no but her continued ill temper will be an added bonus.

Suddenly Raju appears with this proposal.

It is imperative that we give a home to a newly-arrived family of refugees. Even without looking at the financial aspect, 'After all, I am rich and do not need the money', Raju seems to think that I should agree on humanitarian grounds.

I look at my wife and say, 'What?'

'What will I say? It is your house', she leaves the word hanging in the air and stops.

'See your sister-in-law? If you can convince her… then I have no problems with getting tenants', I say to Raju.

'My sister-in-law? Are you talking about Boudi saying no to this?'

Raju seems to have found a way to solve the problem. He sounds relieved and says, 'How can she ever say no? Is she not a mother herself? If she sees the sad faces of those shamed, tormented, unfortunates who have lost everything she will not be able to refuse them.'

'Then it is best that I do not see their faces.'

The passion in Raju's words is doused by Amiya's decisiveness.

'You don't understand sister-in-law, I mean you are not even trying to understand what a terrible state they are in. Can you imagine how desperate people must be to up and leave the land of their ancestors with no hope of ever finding stability?'

'The same thing happened during the bombings',

Amiya is not one for wasting time and so she gathers her wool and knitting needles before sitting down to a drawn out argument. After counting the stitches calmly she says, 'I saw the herd mentality of "desperate" people when the bombs fell. No one seemed to be in their right mind anymore.'

'Herd mentality!'

Raju looks at her wide eyed with amazement and says, 'You want to dismiss bombs as just one of those things? Bombs that can wipe out an entire country in a minute!'

'Of course, that can happen as well. But that is not the point. The point is that people left everything behind and how easily. No real thought went into anything, people just dropped everything and scattered, people from Burdwan going to Hugli and those from Hugli going to Burdwan. Did you not see that too?'

I quickly intervene, not wishing to see Raju cornered so quickly.

'But surely you must see that people can become erratic in the face of great danger?'

Amiya counts the stitches with great concentration and says, 'That they do. That is why they "up and leave" everything and try to save themselves first. Do you remember what one of your aunts did? It was the month of Poush and the day was dedicated to Lakshmi – but your aunt who had always been held up as a role model of a housewife decided to leave all the stuff under the stairs and run away. And yet over here, there was no a whisper about bombs. So we stayed and what happened? Nothing of course.'

Raju must have been sifting through his stock to find a few more impressive sounding words for he started again with a fresh sense of importance, 'But this is not simply a question of life. It is a question of honour as well. What is life compared to honour? Like an anthill compared to the mighty Himalayas! The poor refugees, reduced to begging on the streets today in an effort to maintain their honour.'

He sighs deeply. Every molecule of exhaled air bears witness to his immense sympathy for those seeking shelter because they have nothing any more.

But Amiya? Even though a woman and a member of that group of humans who are mothers, she does not show a glimmer of sympathy. She says quite easily, 'For honour and so on! How clever is it to leave home with your family with no guarantee of what may happen on the journey?'

Raju seems to wince from genuine pain as he says, 'You? You are saying such cruel things? Try and remember that poem by Tagore.'

'Poem by Tagore?'

Amiya covers her mouth and laughs; 'This is new indeed from the likes of you! You taking Tagore's name? But which particular poem might you be referring to that gives good advice regarding cruelty?'

'Aha, shei je, something, something, do you not

remember? What kind of a Tagore fan are you? Such a famous poem and you cannot remember it!'

'How can I remember, at least give me one line to work with.'

'That poem, ah! I have remembered it now: If the motherless do not receive then what celebration is it today! We had it in our Matriculation selection. Such a long time ago too!'

I was amazed, 'But this is not really the same thing is it? Does it fit your point of view?'

'Does not fit? What are you saying?' Raju starts again with fresh enthusiasm.

'Suppose, "If the homeless do not receive, then what is this self rule?" Does it fit now? These thousands of homeless who are spreading like floodwaters across the roads and lesser lanes of India, if they do not find shelter then of what use is this freedom?'

I was softening at his words… truly, of what use was independence, of what good was self-rule if thousands had to live on the street. I was about to agree when Amiya laughed again, 'The comparison is not bad at all, but do you know what happens when you let floodwaters into your home?'

'You know what has happened to people like you; you have been suspicious for so long that you have forgotten what it is like to trust. But let that be.'

Raju continues forcefully, 'You must give up the ground floor or else an entire family will be ruined. If you give just a little you will rescue a family from disaster and yet you will not show a little compassion?'

'This is too much! Why, where are they living at the moment? At the station or on the pavement?' Amiya says with some annoyance.

'For the time being they are living in our house, but that can hardly be a permanent solution. They came because of a link with my father – they were childhood friends. They appeared on our doorstep one day, do you understand how much they must be suffering in our little house? I don't think I can impress upon you how...' Raju said quickly.

'You do not have to impress me anymore, I understand perfectly. But I will not rent our house to people from East Bengal, I am telling you right now.'

'East Bengal? What country is that then? Where will you find East Bengal on an atlas? Even if you had said East Pakistan I would understand. But why this dislike of people of that country?' Raju sounds as if Amiya has spoken in Telugu to him.

This time Amiya has to say what her real reason for dislike is. She says, 'They are really dirty people!'

'Is that all?'

This time it is Raju's turn to smile. 'Is that the reason why you kept saying no? Are they going to forcibly cook the offerings for your altar?'

'They will make the whole house dirty! You do not know, they are so terribly...'

I have to intervene this time. I scold Amiya and say, 'What kind of talk is that? Just because you saw something once does not mean the whole race is to be blamed. Why, I think, if you listen to your conscience, well how much rent are they going to pay?'

'Rent?' Raju jumps up. 'Do not worry about that at all. Whatever you say will go – of course I have told them the rent will be a hundred and thirty, but if you want I will convince them to give a hundred and fifty in full. Do not worry about rent, just say yes. I am of course referring to my sister, can I say yes to them then?'

Just as Amiya is about to say no, Raju hushes her and says, 'Enough, good lady, for the sake of humanity, do not disappoint these poor refugees. I promise you, they will go as soon as they find another house. Let them stay here in the meantime.'

Amiya says, a little reassured perhaps, 'They will go soon?'

'That is what I said, as soon as they find another house.'

'Alright then!'

She sounds as if she was not happy about the situation.

I have to admit though, I cannot lie... I was quite thrilled secretly. A hundred and fifty rupees! That meant that a few unused rooms would pay for the monthly shopping. Who would not be happy at this thought?

They will go as soon as they find another house? Well, I would worry about that when the day came. As the saying goes, 'Why worry about the oil when Radha may not agree to dance!'

Raju did not say another word. He got up suddenly and unbelievably came back within forty five minutes with two push carts and six rickshaws.

ARE you wondering why Raju needed so many things to transport himself? But he was just the guide; the people who needed to be transported were also there with him.

Eighteen people of different sizes and a couple of children descended rapidly from the six rickshaws before our stupefied gazes.

Do you want to know about the two pushcarts? Do you wish to find out what was loaded on them? Instead, let me list what they did not carry.

What was not on those two carts? Mortar and pestles, knives and other sharp blades, baskets and lids, pots and buckets, boxes and bedding, cane swings, metal chairs, wooden beds, earthenware ovens, bags of coal, baskets of cow dung cakes for fuel, coconut shells, copra, brooms and mops, door mats, hand fans – and other paraphernalia of household life. What else did they have? Broken cycles? A pram without wheels? A gramophone with a battered trumpet? Red aquarium fish? A parrot? A puppy?

What did they not have?

We go silent at the sight of this family who were said to have left all their things behind in another land in a hurry to save themselves and their honour.

Amiya looks at me and I look at her again and again. But this is not the meeting of eyes across the holy fire during a marriage, there is no love shining in these glances. My eyes are dark with guilt while hers burn with anger.

Is she angry?

Have flames ever gone out when there is a favourable breeze blowing towards them?

As the days pass, I forget that Amiya ever knew how to smile. Her beloved wool rolls in the dust and the needles rust. She has no time to think of them anymore. Does she have time to think of anyone?

Except for the refugees who have lost everything and are now sheltering on our first floor.

'Son of a bitch had a great wish to rent these rooms out! He had great hopes of getting hundred and fifty rupees as rent! I will see what fool pays him so much rent! He has not met people from Naraangunje before! I will relinquish this house but I will take him down with me!'

These well-constructed words need no stairway to ascend upwards, they fly in the air.

Then the burning eyes bore into my very soul, 'Did you hear that? Do you believe me now? Are you still suspicious that I may be making all this up? Every day, do you understand? And it is increasing each time!'

'But why?'

I sound guilty.

'Why? Because the house is small and they only get the use of a few rooms, their enormous household does not fit here.'

'What do they mean by a few rooms? They knew how many they would have when they came here.'

'What is the point of saying that? They have lost everything so we must give everything up for them. Isn't that our responsibility?'

'What next! The other day they forcibly took possession of the room on the landing, they still need more space?'

'Need more space? This is not an urban Calcuttan like you with one wife and one child all year round. Don't these people have relatives? There are eleven relatives living with the eighteen that are our tenants, how are they supposed to fit? For the lack of sleeping space, "brudda-in-laws are having to sleep in the same room as the sista-in-laws", that is our fault too! So many other demands! Separate kitchens for nonvegetarian and vegetarian foods! Separate bathrooms for men and women, I can't even understand half the words they say. When they speak it is like a storm is raging.'

'They cannot insult us like this! This cannot go on', I venture after some careful thought.

'Cannot go on? Hmmph! Why do you not listen to

what they are saying and then see whether it cannot go on?'

I try listening and soon every hair stands on end.

The words come sailing through the air like an armada at war.

'Yes! Yes! No need to warn us to be careful! So what if they are the landlords! What will they do to me, eh? Will he hang me? I will say whatever I want! Why does the bastard hide with his wife in the corner of his room? Let him come downstairs once and face me! We men from Narayangunge do not fear a bit of bloodshed! What did you say? Police? What will they do to me? Collecting a hundred and fifty from one and half rooms – what a shark! May be he will see sense once he is biting the dust!'

'Amiya?'

'Yes?'

'What are they saying?'

'Well, does the master now believe the humble wife?'

'No, this is really the limit! Who do they think they are?'

I almost run to the phone and dial the number.

Two three two one…Burrabazar – 'Who is that? Raju? Such good luck! I am asking you to come here as soon as you can. What did you say? What is the urgency? Do you not know what kind of dangerous people you have installed in our house? What do you mean, but still? They are cursing us all the time! All you can ask is "Why?"'

'No reason except the fact that the house is small. I cannot say everything on the phone, just come over. What are you saying? You don't even have time to take a break! Since when have you been so busy? All pretences for sure! But you must come and solve the problem!'

I count the days in the hopes of a solution but Raju fails to show up.

In the meantime the situation goes from bad to worse.

I call the number again. 'Hello, hello? Is that Raju? Praise the Lord! What happened to your coming over? "No time!" You are busy trying to resettle all the refugees? How many people have you tricked into doing what I did? I do not want to hear any excuses! Take these people somewhere else! What are you saying? You call me mad! That is not impossible at all; in fact, it is very possible that I have gone mad! Come and find out!'

But where is Raju's thirst for knowledge? So I call him again, forgetting all my dignity, 'Raju, we are finished! What are you doing? Why are you not coming to our house? You are? This is not another excuse? Okay, I will wait for you to turn up then.'

A few more days pass in waiting. Eventually the day I return from work to find my son with a bandaged head, I go off in search of Raju. As I pull my shirt on and walk down the stairs, I hear Raju's voice.

He sounds like he is trying to assure someone as he walks upstairs.

We collide on the stairs.

'So, finally you have made time to come and see us.'

'Made time? I do not have the time to catch a breath! I had to… Tejeshbabu had called me just a while ago, he had a complaint…'

'Oh, really? So what was the great Tejeshbabu's complaint?'

'He was saying … apparently it has been an ongoing thing, I did not believe him of course. But apparently, they have been at the receiving end of a lot of misbehavior. Your wife threatens them with eviction, how wrong is that? The poor fellows are without shelter, they have found this roof after so much hardship. What is the meaning of these threats?'

'What do you mean they have found this roof? Are you trying to say that they will live here forever?'

'What else will they do?'

'Even after cracking my son's skull open?'

'Shame on you for saying it like that', Raju responded as though he had himself been struck.

'I heard what happened from them, you are simply making mountains out of a very small molehill. Children fight all the time , who holds it against them?'

'Raju?' an ominous call comes from above.

'Oh, my sister? Greetings!'

'That is enough. Tell me, what of their housing? Have you found them something?'

'Housing? Where will they find a house?'

Raju stares at her as if Amiya had asked him for the moon.

'You had promised they would leave soon.'

'I admit that I did say that, but where will they go? They are living under a lot of stress here as well. They had a two storey house back home, one might go as far as calling it a mansion. To have to leave all that and live like this....'

'So why leave that palatial mansion?'

'Fate!'

'I do not understand what you mean, just get rid of them!'

'How can I do that? What have they done?'

'Firstly, they have committed theft.'

'Theft?'

'Yes, that is what it is called in plainspeak! Clothes hung out at night on the railings are gone by morning!'

'Is that all? They probably got blown away in the wind!'

'I have been hanging washing there all my life and three sarees simply get blown away as soon as these people arrive?'

'Why is that so amazing? Don't people die suddenly after living a long life? If you are not careful, you may have thirty sarees blown away by a strong wind!'

'Wonderful! And how do they end up on the women downstairs?'

'This is really very wrong of you! There are more than one saree of each design in the markets.'

'Stop talking rubbish! How can I not recognise my own belongings? Women can find their own things even when they are dead and have come back as ghosts, you know! Are we to live with thieves?'

'Now, now, it could be that they are using the sarees without knowing who they belong to.'

'Wonderful! And what of the fact that my pots and pans seem to be ending up in their kitchen? Is that the fault of the wind too? Let me go and show you where my large bowl, my brass pot, three of my engraved glasses....'

'This is all your anger talking; do you not know how wealthy they were? They left nearly two trunks filled with such pots and pans back home. Today you accuse them of pilfering a bowl or two....'

'Of course that is normal, the easiest thing for people to do is to fill an empty space. If I was to die today, your brother would rush to get a scarecrow to fill the emptiness....'

'Why drag me into your conversation? Just stick to the matter at hand', I protest.

'The conversation is utterly useless. I cannot do what she is asking in anger. Well, I will be off. Take care that you behave in a kindly manner with them, at least look to your conscience and do the right thing', Raju says.

I say with annoyance, 'What are you saying? If you heard how they curse us....'

'They don't do that without reason. They do it under duress. That was what Tejeshbabu was saying – how they have to divide the room with three separate mosquito nets to keep privacy. But you could have helped if only you had wanted to!'

'Me?'

I am astonished.

'Yes, you. And your wife; see how you have four rooms on the second floor that are not really being put to use? If only you move into one room with your family and let them have the other three….'

The second floor too?

I stop him before he can go further and say, 'Do not anger your sister any more Raju, just try to find a way for them to leave.'

'I know you will not let them have the rooms. If only people were kinder, the refugees from East Pakistan would not have been in such dire straits. At least for the sake of humanity….-'

'Please, less of those excuses. Tell us if you can find them other accommodation….'

'Impossible.'

'Impossible? Are you trying to say that they will live here forever?'

'What to do? They are refugees….'

'But do we have to put up with this torment for just that reason?'

'Do not think of it as torment and things will be much easier.'

'What? What do you mean do not think of it? They are pilfering things from our home and we must keep quiet about it?' Amiya reddens with anger.

'What else can you do? It will only add fuel to the argument if you speak up.'

'Their boy will hit my child hard enough to make him bleed, but we must keep quiet about it?'

'Well, what can you say? It was an accident of course! It could just as easily have been the opposite. What if he had injured himself in a fall on the stairs? What would you do then?'

'Great! Then why hang people for murder? It is best to explain it away as natural death!'

'Truly, when will such a day dawn on this earth?'

I try to impress Raju into silence and say, 'Just fights among the boys? They call his father all kinds of names, from bastard to bastard's son!'

'Please do not pay attention to that! It is not really hurting you, is it? You can see it is the result of poor upbringing!'

'We do not care what results from what! We will have to take the help of legal channels if it comes to that.'

'Law? You will take legal help to oust refugees? Even the government has given up on that!' Raju roars with laughter.

'So they will continue to rip us off and we will go on saying "Poor refugees!" as long we have to.'

'But sister, that is the meaning of humanity.'

'Blast humanity! I promise you I will drive them out!'

'Are you mad? Please do not even tread on that path! You have no idea how angry those people from the other side of the river can get, you are used to living with meek fellows like us. Plus the tenancy laws are also very convoluted.'

'Tenants? When did we get tenants Raju? I am yet to see a single coin in the two months that they have been here. The first month they said they would pay us the next month and then it became the month after. Now they openly say they "would rather give us horse eggs than real money"! You turned out to be some wellwisher!' I could not help saying.

Suddenly Raju's expression changes completely and a guilty look comes over him as he says, 'What can I do Dibu, my heart breaks at their misfortune. Would they not pay rent if they could? But they cannot, can they? Poor helpless refugees! Driven from their own homes. Does your heart not weep when you look at them? How can you think of things as banal as money?'

Foot Soldiers

(Pawdatik)

Unbearable! Unbearable!

Savitri has started again – her monotonous moaning. A strange blend of exhaustion and sharp words – 'I cannot do this anymore! I will be happy when it is my time! So many people die each day, why won't death take me?'

Every day.

She complains about accursed Death every day. She complains about her inabilities every day. As if it is not enough unless all the people living around them have been made aware that death is the only way out for her.

Jayanti finds this so very ugly. She finds it unbearable.

She does not feel like addressing her mother as 'Ma' any more. All links to the house are gradually being erased except for eating hand rolled bread twice a day and sheltering at night. Jayanti is erasing them on purpose, she has already stopped having tea or breakfast at home.

She does not have the time to turn up for four meals a day.

She does not try to make time either.

But she still has to return once a day to the house. She has to return – to fling herself into bed, her exhausted body crushed by the relentless drudgery of the day.

Savitri starts to complain and regret as soon as she steps into the house.

Or perhaps she does not start, she merely continues what she has been doing all day long. Jayanti is not at home the whole day, so she does not get to hear any of it. Thank God for that, she would surely have gone mad if that had not been the case.

All she has to do is to cook for a few people – why does this irritate Savitri so much? Why is she so incapable? It is not as if she has to go out and make the money to pay for the meals either!

The kind of back-breaking labour Jayanti has to undergo! Has anyone thought about that once? Can Savitri not see that from a human viewpoint at least, if not from the gentleness of a maternal soul? Does her conscience not stop her from pouring out these shameless complaints and constant angry rants against death and God into the ears of a daughter who is working herself into the ground to keep the household going?

There is no saying anything to her as she then loses it completely in a flood of tears.

It is best to remain quiet.

Jayanti is growing more and more distant as she tries to keep from speaking out. When the rains come suddenly, she sits and watches in silence these days as the clothes on the line grow wet again.

She is no longer perturbed by the unfortunate event of dry clothes getting wet in this needy household where no one ever has enough to wear. There is a sort of cruel revenge that gathers within her these days. Not against fate but against her mother.

At least if it was a household worth doing something for. What ugliness!

The young children are a miserable lot. They are not properly clothed, their hair is not combed neatly, they do not get food on time, they are unloved even when they are ill, they are growing up like children living in slums – in dust, mud, algae.

When Jayanti and her father sit down to eat rice at lunch, it is like thieves. And to what sort of meal? If there is dal to go with the rice they must count it as enough. Instead of being apologetic as she pushes burning hot half cooked rice and dal towards them, Savitri lists everything that make it hard for her to cook for them before even the crows have woken up. She does not forget to state that she could have made a couple of dishes to go with the rice if she had just a little more time. It is all because of their rushing about that….

As if a couple of dishes would have eased her father Bijanbabu's passage to heaven and that of Jayanti with him. As if nine o'clock is too early; what does she do with her time anyway, she is always up before the sun! What does she do all this time! Peculiar!

Jayanti wakes so much later and manages to tutor at two places before nine o'clock. Her father does tutoring, the daily shopping, collects their rations, buys the coal – a hundred things that no one else can do.

Neither of them are calling on death for deliverance, are they?

Jayanti does not even feel like eating today.

As she came home from her tutoring, she saw Savitri beating her youngest child and screaming for both to be taken from this world. There was no way of knowing what he had done that was so wrong as he was not old enough to speak.

As she climbes the stairs to seek refuge in her own bed, Jayanti tries to imagine the degree of cruelty in her mother's nature that makes her hit a two-year-old child again and again with all her strength.

When little Meenu comes a little later with a cup of tea and places it in front of Jayanti with the greatest concentration, Jayanti commands, 'Go tell her I will not eat anything! Throw this tea away!'

On other days this would have led to a round of irritating requests but today no one comes back to annoy her even further.

Who would do it anyway?

Savitri seems to have totally lost it today.

IT is not as if Jayanti falls asleep as soon as she lies down. She lies there listening as Savitri screaming, her younger brothers and sisters cry, spices sizzle. Screaming that does not stop, a tirade against her husband, against the gods, against her timid husband, her educated eldest daughter, against the entire universe.

Savitri shouts, 'So much money is spent on this household, can someone not buy a length of rope for five paise? Just buy one and deliver me from this wretched family! But why would you buy anything for me? That would mean being arrest for you, wouldn't it? Instead, let me die a little at a time.'

'What? You are feeling hungry again? Get out! Get out! Out of my sight, you wretch!'

'Why do you not eat my flesh! If you are always so hungry, why come to a needy family?'

These and a thousand other beautiful words pour out of Savitri like a flood.

Unbearable! Unbearable!

'Father', Jayanti eventually goes to the other room.

'It is unbearable. I do not think it is possible to live in this house.'

Startled, her father sits up. He takes a look at her face, his eyes questioning.

'Perhaps you can block your ears to this after hearing it all the time, but I cannot do this anymore; I must find some other place to live in.'

Bijanbabu says in slightly pained tones, 'I think she is going a little mad these days. She works so hard too. Ever since the maid left'.

Jayanti retorts, 'Just boiling up some rice and dal is hardly the toughest job in the world Father, who gets to put food in their mouth without working for it anyway? But there should be a limit to her temper. She is not really mad after all!'

Bijanbabu seems to be compensating for his wife's unkindness as his voice grows even more subdued; 'Truly, she has become so, what is the word for it? What can I say, anything will bring things to a head!'

'That same fear has silenced me too father, but it is getting harder. Something must be done.'

'What else can be done? Just get rid of me! What can I do? Even death won't have me!' Neither had noticed Savitri come and stand behind them. Her words are flung from the darkness at the door, 'I call on it all day to come and get me. But will it listen to me?'

Jayanti feels irritated at this attempt to pick a fight, her eyes fill with a mixture of disgust, hate and indifference and she walks away without a word; Savitri asks, 'And why will you not be eating?'

This is the spark that she needed. Flaring up, Jayanti answers bitterly, 'I do not wish to eat in this house anymore Ma....'

'What! What did you say? No wish to eat? You do not wish to eat because I cook? Why? Because I am uneducated? Because I cannot walk around in socks and shoes like you lot? What is the reason?'

'No reason Ma, none at all! But I beg you all, can I please have some peace at least today? I will be the one that leaves, I promise!'

She says these words cuttingly and goes to her room where she waits; for another storm of annoying words. But strangely enough, it is as if the house has fallen under a spell of silence. As if a machine has fallen quiet after some sort of breakdown.

After thinking about a lot of things while she lies in bed, Jayanti remembers that there is a union meeting the following day. Everyone is insisting that she say a few words there. If she cannot manage an extempore speech, at least read from one prepared earlier. She should have done a draft last night. But with all this going on, it was hardly possible. At least the next day was a Saturday and the meeting was not till five, so she would be able to get something ready. She might even go straight to the secretary's house to do it. After all, this house is hardly the place to do work. The secretary, Salil Sen, had told her a few points that she could include in her speech. He thinks that women make more effective leaders and that was why he had asked Jayanti to speak.

The points swirled through her brain.

The ideas were all old however; they just had to be presented in a new way. The same old conflict between bosses and workers. A struggle against the differences between those who count and the uncounted masses; the question that they must ask – 'The innumerable foot soldiers who fought in the struggle for freedom, who died in it, who supplied labour and food, has darkness been lifted from their world? Who has the responsibility of remembering them? The history books will note the names of the generals in letters of gold, but as we read of their sacrifices and focus, of their struggles and their incarceration, will anyone recall for once the nameless and miserable foot soldiers? The ones who have lost everything in this battle?'

The gentleman had rolled out a great many words like these, dampened with much emotion. She would be able to write them all down if she let her mind calm down before she sat with pen and paper.

But when she calmed down she fell asleep.

Would Salil Sen understand the horrible environment Jayanti had to live in?

HOW long had she slept?

Was it two hours or ten hours? She must have slept for ages; why else would her father wake her suddenly with that anxious cry?

'Jaya, Jaya! Wake up! Your mother is behaving very strangely. I have to go and get the doctor, Jaya!'

What was mother behaving like?

What kind of language was this?

'Behaving strangely' – what does that mean?

Jayanti sits up with a start and stares at him stupidly.

As he puts his vest on, Bijanbabu's voice cracks as he says, 'But will the doctor be of any use? Perhaps she is dead by now. She is not making any sounds and I could not find a pulse. Can you be a brave girl and sit with her for a while? Let me go and find the doctor. God knows if he will agree to come along. What a thing to happen while getting a drink! I cannot tell whether she fell after fainting or fainted as a result of the fall!'

He forgets to put his shoes on and walks out barefoot.

The doctor comes, thank God.

But who is he supposed to treat? Can one treat a thing of stone? Science is still at a loss here.

He can only use a set of numbers to indicate that Savitri's blood pressure had been dangerously elevated.

When did the blood pressure go up so much in that thin, anemic, bloodless body of hers? When did it get the chance? Why did no one know till the pressure of her boiling blood ruptured the blood vessels in her brain? But would it have helped if they had known?

What a strange illness!

Nothing to do but wait for the end to come.

There is no chance of running around or doing things for the patient. Perhaps if they had been rich there would have been a series of futile attempts at finding a cure, but those luxuries are not for the poor.

Therefore, Bijanbabu does nothing else but sit at her bedside. Let morning come, he will call on the doctor once again, what more can he do anyway?

But just because Savitri's senses have all become stilled does not mean that the rest of the family have lost their feelings too. Actually, the strain of being awake all night has meant that Bijan babu craves his morning tea even more than other days, as does Jayanti. The younger children begin crying as they wake up. More than they usually do.

They probably like the environment even less today.

At one point, Bijanbabu forgoes all shame and says to Jayanti, 'Why don't you try lighting the clay oven? The children will need to be fed. And some tea....'

Jayanti does not think once of going to work.

She seems to wake up from a stupor; true, she must be the one to do all that today!

But when she goes to the kitchen, she is stunned to see its state.

Where will she strike a match? Will she set her clothes on fire? The oven is full of ash and old coals. Where did they need to be thrown away? Piles of unwashed dishes sit here and there punctuated by the low wooden seats which have also not been put away. Two glasses lie on the ground, witness to Meenu and Shanu's battles of yesterday.

It is obvious that Savitri could not clean the room last night. She starts on her work for the following day late at night, after the whole house has gone quiet.

Cleaning the dishes, sweeping the yard, breaking the coal into small pieces ready for the oven, chopping the vegetables and grinding the spices. As quietly as possible, in as little light as possible – so that no one is woken up, so that she does not use too much kerosene in the lamps.

Did Jayanti ever remember seeing when Savitri finally came to bed?

But there is no point in thinking of Savitri now, she has turned away from life today – perhaps as revenge on Jayanti.

Now what will Jayanti do?

Will she clean these dishes? Will she wash the room down with water? Will she throw away the ashes and stoke the fire again with new coal, wood and cow dung cakes? What will she do once the fire is lit? Only tea? Rice and dal? Barley in milk? Now? Later? At night?

Thwarted from having tea, Bijanbabu slips away at one stage on the pretext of getting the children some food and has a cup of tea at the shops. Even though his mind sinks at the thought of Savitri's condition, he cannot forgo his tea. He raises the empty cup to his lips absentmindedly as he thinks of how she will never wake him again in the mornings with a big glass of steaming hot tea. His reverie is broken by the gentleman next to him who says, 'Why not have another cup? It is a wet day, hey, give the gentleman another cup of tea….'

'No, no! Let it be!' Bijanbabu says as he gets up in a hurry.

But what has happened to Jayanti?

The minute they digest the puffed rice, Khoka and Chandu, both begin hankering for rice. Bijanbabu puts up with it for a while before going to his daughter again. He asks hesitantly, 'Is the rice done Jaya? If it is, then just give them plain rice with a drop of milk. I cannot manage them any more.'

Rice? Is he dreaming?

Jayanti has just finished cleaning the dishes, there are piles of clothes to be washed and the municipal tap just dried up for the day.

Meenu had lit the oven out of the kindness of her heart for her sister, but who can tell why it went out after belching a lot of smoke. Now Jayanti stands with a fan, feeling useless. She did not store one drop of water, what can she cook the rice in?

At this point comes her father's question; 'Is the rice done?'

How will the rice be done? Amazing.

She seethes at her father's lack of consideration but there is little she can say. It is true that it is half past ten already.

There might not be any ponds in Calcutta but there are many tube wells; signs of the benevolence of the government; faint remnants of the time when the city had been at war. Meenu does about fifteen trips to fetch water with a little bucket.

That saves the day.

But Jayanti has no idea how it got to be two o'clock before she can put plates of rice and dal in front of the family.

By the time she finished eating, it would be three o'clock and then she would have to wash the kitchen floors and sweep the rest of the house. She would have to do the dishes and wash all the clothes that had collected over the day, a ragged collection. Then the oven; the rice and the dal again; then, after it was all done she would start preparing for the next day. Without that preparation, it would be just as chaotic again. Jayanti realises that she does not even know what else needs to be done.

Tomorrow...then the day after, and the day after that. Day after day after day – Savitri would never shoulder this load ever again. Nor would she ever come down the stairs on her own. After lying like a thing of stone in silence, she would be silenced forever. Someone else would carry her down.

WHO will do all this?

Jayanti feels like taking to her bed in exhaustion just from doing this once. She feels like running away from home. What about doing it again, and again?

Bijanbabu must have felt pity on seeing Jayanti's expression, for in the afternoon he said, 'Jaya, listen, there is no need to think about cooking anything this evening. Let us make do with bread from the shops and you go sit with your mother now while I try to make some tea.'

'You? What will you do?' Jayanti says miserably.

'Let me see. We are both equally new to this. Meenu, come with me and show me where everything is.'

Jayanti stands and watches quietly even as her father tries to light the oven. She has no wish to stop him; soon she goes to her mother and sits on the edge of the bed.

Savitri is lying there, her face expressionless, as if she has renounced the world without waiting for death to remove her from it first.

Is Jayanti crying because of her anguish for her mother?

Savitri has managed for all this time with this lean skeletal frame. Day after day and night after night. But they never had to make do with bread from the shops. Meenu never had to walk to the tubewell for water either.

When had she ever seen her father squatting on the kitchen floor trying to get the oven going?

Had she ever done a thing in the kitchen since she had found a job?

How much was her salary worth? Or was it so important to her that she lost sight of the important things?

The clock suddenly struck five.

Five o'clock. What was she meant to do at five o'clock? Oh, the meeting. She had not even gone to work today. She had not thought of it all this time. What was she meant to say? She could not remember Salil Sen's face at all. But some of the things he had said came to mind. What was a foot soldier again? Who were they? Was it only those who were factory workers?

Freedom, But At What Cost

(Swadhinotar Shukh)

Chanchala has been having a great time ever since her elder sister Ujwala moved to this neighbourhood. She feels so grateful to have her sister close by.

Their parents stay far away and meetings with them are occasional. Poor Chanchala has been stuck with her in-laws ever since her marriage, almost as if she had become part of the furniture of the house. She had almost forgotten that she had another family once.

Ujwala did not live that far away, she was only in Howrah on the other side of the city where her in-laws lived but they did not meet that often despite the proximity. They were both creatures living in captivity.

But now Ujwala has found freedom. She has left the old house behind and bought a house in this neighbourhood.

Chanchala feels like she has finally managed to hold the moon in her hands. As the saying goes, 'Mothers and sisters'. Who else will love a woman as much as her sister will? Sisters-in-law? Mother-in-law? If that were true, why then the earth would have been heaven!

Ujwala says words to this effect whenever she comes to see Chanchala.

She frequently takes a rickshaw after lunch and comes to her sister with containers packed with things to eat and stays the rest of the day; leaving when it is almost dark, close to the time when her husband comes home from work. This is also the time when Chanchala's husband Taposh comes home from his job as a school teacher. He finishes at half past four.

That he feels quite blessed to have his rich sister-in-law visit them goes without saying. It is always a matter of great fortune when a well-to-do government employee's wife favours a school teacher's wife because they are sisters.

Quite often when Ujwala is preparing to leave, she casts an eye at her brother-in-law by way of both greeting and farewell and says with a sigh, 'Brother, do take care of your wife, you can see how she is getting worse each day? Who else but you will notice her plight in this family? Cooking for this enormous family in that condition – I worry that she will fall really ill one day. Who else will her death affect? Only you, and us. But we are both her family and not her nearest at the same time. We do not really have any rights to say anything.'

She has a way with these honeyed words, drawing them

out so that her brother-in-law hears them all before she leaves for home.

Embarrassed, slightly guilty, Taposh looks at his wife closely but cannot see what deterioration there has been in Chanchala's 'plight' lately. She has always been a slender person, any weight she puts on is simply like laying a pebble on its side instead of standing it up. But she is very strong. She works easily at all the household chores. The poor schoolmaster has never thought it part of his responsibility to express concern at his wife's condition.

At first he used to ask Chanchala about this with a sense of misgiving, but she laughed it off. She answered, 'Don't pay attention to my sister! She always thinks I am getting thinner. If I really was getting thinner at that rate I would have evaporated by now, don't you think?'

These days he has learned to ignore Ujwala's remarks and not ask Chanchala any questions. She freely answers her sister these days, saying 'Why are you wasting your breath sister? No one cares whether I live or die. But you notice because you are my own sister. Do you think anyone else in this household gives it a second thought? It is all for show – youngest daughter-in-law and all that! It is all self-interest! I work in silence like a donkey, that is enough! Who cares how hard I work? The day I fall ill, they will throw me out like so much rubbish!'

As he hears her talk, Taposh feels very uncomfortable. It seems that her words are becoming harsher and ruder as each day passes. Did she use such uncivilised speech before? Especially in front of others?

But even after her sister leaves Taposh says nothing about this, he is growing shrewd each day. He knows that she will lash out if he says anything. But why is she becoming so impatient lately? Is this really a sign of some internal illness? Previously everyone used to praise her sweet nature and her smiling face. His brother, his sister, even the domestic helpers are completely under her spell.

His mother has nothing but good things to say about her youngest daughter-in-law! The nephews and nieces are all devoted to their youngest aunt! Who does not love Chanchala? But lately there is a distinct ebb in the love. Even Taposh with all his inexperience notices this.

But why? Is she right then? Are all relationships bound up in self-interest? She could work tirelessly and take care of everyone without a break – from the oldest to the youngest in the house, was that why they showered her with so much love and affection? Now her health is not as good as before, nor is she as strong and the need to love her has decreased – could it be true? But Taposh does not really see any lessening in strength or any ill health; it is hard for him to make a decision either way.

But the one thing he cannot deny is that the hitherto docile Chanchala is quite vocal these days. It is as if she is always looking for an opportunity to give people a piece of her mind. Like a snake constantly poised to strike.

Now, why shouldn't that be? Are people supposed to be ignorant of their rights at all times? Are they to provide an opportunity for others to trick them when possible? She got married young and has been confined under this roof since then. She did not know any better and felt happy with the praise that people showered on her. It was only after her sister's arrival that Chanchala began to really see how she had been working with nothing to show for it all this time. How she has poured fuel into ashes!

Why just Chanchala, consider Taposh as well? It might sound like he is a mere school teacher, but he makes quite a bit when you count all the tutoring after school and payments for marking examinations. They have hardly any expenses themselves. Chanchala and their two young daughters – they make up Taposh's family. But everything he makes goes into the giant maw of the household.

At first Ujwala was astounded to hear this. She had said, 'What are you saying? He gives everything he earns to his mother? He does not save anything? Shame on him! I have to say though, just because he has lost his mind does not mean you have to do the same? Don't you think about your own interests? You must think of these things. Take a look at me. The reason your brother-in-law can go about with his head held high is because I thought things through. What would have happened if I had spent everything on his enormous family like you do here? But then, you always were the silly one!'

One can put up with a lot of things, but to be called silly is nothing to be proud of. Shame and self-pity make Chanchala desperate to prove that she is not silly.

She took Taposh down a few notches that day too.

After all, it was Taposh's money; so why should it come to her from her eldest brother-in-law, second handed as it were and as a mark of the older man's generosity? Why? Why such belittlement? Why does she have to go to her sister-in-law and plead like a child for money when her daughter's Horlicks is over? And her proud sister-in-law smiles her biggest smile and says, 'You don't have to tell me youngest wife, go and see how he has put the jar on your table already. He hurried to the shops as soon as he saw you rinsing out the empty bottle.'

As a sister-in-law, she is meant to show her happiness and amazement at her brother-in-law's affection and good sense! She had done so faithfully all this time. But she did it only because she was extremely 'silly'. She does not like pretending any more.

Does Taposh not know where the shops are?

He should keep the money he makes after giving enough to pay for their family's needs. He should try and save some of the money.

She had to argue so much with Taposh to get him to agree to that arrangement. But still, happiness eludes her.

WHERE will happiness come from if there is no freedom?

There are three masters and five mistresses over the two of them. What a great situation! Will the rays of freedom ever cross those mountains and light up the darkness that is Chanchala's life?

Ujwala said it even today as she left, 'What can you do, your husbard is such a simpleton! If you followed my instructions there is no need for any unhappiness at all! Your brother-in-law was saying that one of his friends has a ground floor for rent. If Taposh takes it, he will not charge the full amount. We know him very well! Well, who is going and who is staying? Our Taposh is completely servile when it comes to his mother and brothers. He just does not understand that everyone is a fair-weather friend, but will they stand by your side when the times are tough? I have seen a lot in this life time. I look out for you because you are my sister. See if you can convince him, if he listens to you. The little ones aside, the two of you will be able to cook, eat, stay smartly turned out at all times, go to the movies, do up your rooms, after all this is the age for all that! Instead of that, all you are doing is preparing tonnes of food for the family at two enormous ovens, no fancies, no wishes fulfilled, no dressing up – why it makes me want to cry. Do you even get to look after your children? Why, the other day I saw the two sitting in the cold downstairs with their cousins and eating bread. Dear Lord! I cannot bear to see children raised in such deplorable conditions!

My boys Buku and Biju are so much older and they still don't know what bread is! I only give them the best buns and sweets always!'

Chanchala thinks, 'Why does the earth not swallow me up at this instant?'

If only the household were smaller, her girls could live on buns and sweets too.

Alas! Why is Taposh so stupid?

But it is not all bad to be living with a stupid person. Because they have gaps in their comprehension, it is easy to fill them with ideas that belong to other people. One just has to keep persevering at it.

Ujwala definitely has the perseverance and Chanchala has inherited it.

Gradually, Taposh sees the light. He too realises to his great dismay that he has truly been a fool all this time, But who is going to keep their eyes shut to the light. Neither do the two of them.

CHANCHALA went to live independently in the ground floor flat owned by her brother-in-law's friend. Taposh went too.

His mother cursed his wife and the other daughters-in-law dried their eyes in secret while his brothers sighed and said nothing.

Some of the younger children were innocent of what

was happening and came to Chanchala, tearfully hugging her and saying, 'Can we come with you, Aunt?' but their mothers pulled them away.

It was not as if Chanchala was not feeling a sense of unease as well; she just wanted to step over the threshold and escape the tentacles of the octopus.

She was so happy when they were in the new house. 'My own household' – how beautiful are those words! Cook what you want, go to the movies as often as you please!

Going to the movies! In the other house that was a full-scale production! First, one had to get permission from the matriarch and she could not stand the idea of films as entertainment. Once that consent had been extracted, the request went to her eldest son. Of course, he never refused these requests but it was still the rule to ask him. It would apparently have been disrespectful to not ask him for his permission. After all that was your share of household work. Even if people did not say anything if you went off without doing all the chores, it was a matter of personal pride. Then came the question of who else would go to the films for there was no question of going as a couple. The elder sisters-in-law had to be invited and if they didn't want to go, it was a certainty that all the nephews and nieces and other younger family members would have to be taken to see the film.

All this, to watch a film.

All because she was the one who liked to watch films.

And how many had she actually watched? Her sister would say quite often, 'What? Don't tell me you have not seen that one? What is wrong with you? If I don't watch a film as soon as it is released, I feel my life is worth nothing!'

Even Chanchala felt that way, but what could she do? So far, her life had mostly been worth nothing. Now, she had finally found the key to truly being alive.

She tells Taposh on the very first night in the new house – 'We are going to watch two films a week from now on.'

Taposh, however, is not in a very happy mood after having left the other house and he answers casually, 'If you can manage to pay for that, then go by all means.'

'I will be able to do that easily! Just watch me! We will only have to buy two tickets now!' Chanchala lets out a sigh of relief. What a wonderful thought! Not having to go and ask anyone's permission any more. What a great burden it is to have elders! Like a weight on one's chest. When people say elders are like the shelter of mountains, they are not halfway off the mark! What are mountains but piles of stones, when you come to think of it?

'You will not go to your tutoring today!' She says playfully, 'You are only allowed to come home with two tickets to the films, understood?'

Taposh does not dislike this playful side to his wife; chances to talk to each other were few at home. He smiles as he says, 'Understood! But I am to absent myself twice a week then?'

'Why not? Just tell them your wife will get angry and stop eating and sleeping if she does not get to see films!'

'Okay, that is what I will tell them!' Taposh smiles as he leaves.

And he does come home with two tickets!

Chanchala rushes to finish her work happily, until a thought makes her turn cold. Where will she leave her daughters while they are watching the film?

She had not thought about this earlier. Neither had Taposh. These questions never arose while they were in the 'other house', where there was always someone to look after the children. But who would do that here?

She comes to her husband and asks him anxiously, 'Where will Pushi and Hashi stay in the evening?'

What a disaster! Where indeed?

They had forgotten all about the children in the joy over having to buy 'just two tickets'! Will two more tickets be available if they take the children along? A romantic evening for the two of them – completely ruined by taking the children!

But what can be done? They cannot be left on their own.

Taposh says somberly, 'We will not go. That is it. What a waste of money!'

Chanchala feels like crying when she hears him say that. How can he be so cruel?

She sulks for a while and then says, 'I am telling you

now, I will never ask to go to another film ever again!'

Taposh says with exasperation, 'Why are you getting angry for no reason? We should have thought of this earlier. Anyway, let us do something. Let us leave them with the landlord's family'.

'Will they agree to have them?'

'Why not? Give them their dinner beforehand.'

That is what they will do then. No matter how angry or sad they feel, greed wins in the end.

Chanchala drags the two girls upstairs. But the landlord's wife refuses immediately, turning her down very pleasantly, with a reasonable, 'How can that be? They hardly know me, why would they agree to stay here? I will have a hard time if they start to cry'.

Chanchala cannot say to her after this, 'Why do I care if you have a hard time?'

But if the landlady had heard what Chanchala says about her once she is downstairs , she would probably have committed suicide in remorse.

The other alternative is to leave them with her sister. That is not a bad idea at all. That is what they do in the end. But needless to say, her sister is not very happy about it at all. They are left with sister and nothing more.

As they get into the rickshaw, Taposh says, 'Your sister was not very happy at all by the way.'

Chanchala knows that too but she will not admit that. She says dismissively, 'What are you saying! How can she not like it? She is their aunt, if she has them over for one day....'

Taposh interrupts, 'Yes, mark my words. It will only be this one day'.

After all this, they find that the show has already started when they get to the hall.

The girls have to be picked up on their way home. Chanchala's sister gives them an exaggerated account of the evening; the gist of it being the fact that she has never seen two little creatures like this in her entire life. What horrible children! Her own children were their age once, she does not remember such behavior from them.

Taposh and Chanchala carry the sleeping girls to the rickshaw with sullen faces.

But are their troubles to end there?

It would have been good for the school teacher if that had been the worst part of the evening. But there is no chance of that.

When they get home, they find the door ajar and the padlock gone.

What does that mean?

He lights a match with great difficulty as he balances a sleeping child on his shoulder. Inside, he lays her on the ground and sits down heavily.

Chanchala is following slowly with the other child; Taposh was meant to go back for this one after he had opened the door. But once she goes into the new place, she begins to cry.

If this was a riddle, I could have ended with a question for you. But since it is not, I will tell you what has happened. Everything they owned had been stolen in the two hours they had been away.

Only the bedclothes and pillows lie strewn about the room.

When Chanchala is calmer, she screams, 'Do you know that the landlord can be taken to the police over this? We left in front of them just as evening was falling....'

Taposh stops her saying, 'Quiet, quiet! Remember, this is your brother-in-law's friend's house. We did not ask them to stand on guard for us now, did we?'

The Theft

(Awporadh)

'Listen to this! Listen to what Niren has written to me!'

Kalyani put the tea cup on the table and asked in astonishment, 'Niren? My brother-n-law? Why has he written to you of all people? What does he say?'

'What he has written makes my head spin!'

'But why? What on earth could he have written?'

'What has he written indeed! There is some kind of literary meet here or some other useless event and that is why he is coming. "But why stay in a hotel when he has a close relative", so he is deigning to set foot in this poor cousin's hovel.'

Kalyani understood why Paresh was angry but still smiled and said, 'It is a matter of happiness that a relative will come on a visit, why are you angry at this?'

'Don't talk rot!' Paresh raised the tea cup from the table and put it back down before saying, 'Do you know that it is the twenty third of the month today, or are you pretending not to?'

'Of course, I know. Even the bones buried inside me know that.'

'Then?'

'What can you do? He says he will come – surely, you cannot ask him not to?'

'Why not? The poor have to be able to do many things. I am writing to him clearly, instead of staying so far from the rest of his group, it will be easier for him to be closer to Calcutta… creature comforts.'

'What! How can you tell him that? He must have considered all that before he wrote to you? He will see straight away that you do not want him to come and stay.'

'What does it matter if he does? How will I manage all that? If it was someone of our sort, it would have been different. Do you not know their standard of living? It is as if there is no pain or want in the whole wide world!'

'Yes, I know that. I have been to your uncle's house a few times, as a new bride. What a beautiful house! What beautiful interiors! Your aunt had so much jewellery on!'

'What about the beautiful pride! The showing off! That aunt of mine never stooped so low as to talk to my mother and the others.'

Kalyani smiled again and said, 'Are you still angry with her for that?'

'No, I am not angry any more. But I do remember it. Of course, Niren and his brother Suren always loved us, but it is what I said – they are blind to the existence of poverty. He will be stupefied at every turn when he sees how we live, what we eat, how we manage – that is all.'

Kalyani was quiet for a few moments before she asked, 'How long will he stay?'

'Who knows? But will it be less than a minimum of one week?'

Paresh finally picks up his tea and finishes it despite a skin of cold…at one go.

Looking at his face you would think he had just swallowed some bitter medicine.

Kalyani comes back after a while and says, 'Look, would you be doing the right thing by asking him not to come? After all, he is family. The shame will last a lifetime. There is such a thing called pride.'

Paresh knows all this, but his blood freezes when he thinks of his pocket book. Only God knows how that final week of each month is eked out. Kalyani might have displayed her own sense by citing pride but there are other things to consider.

It is quite possible that Niren spends the same amount in a month on just cigarettes that Paresh spends in the entire month on running his entire household. He could quite easily be spending more in fact. Even hosting him under their roof for seven days might be difficult. There would have to be some standards that they would have to maintain. How much did those standards cost?

Everything they wore, every bed and every pillow would need to be given a veneer of respectability. The family would have to be given everything that the guest was offered. Everything, from the hair oil and toothpaste they used to the tea cups they drank from would need to have the general air of poverty and dilapidation erased from them; who knows how much that would all cost?

And if they chose to do nothing to hide the real shape of their poverty and presented themselves as needy, that was a different matter. Niren might feel compassion and even offer some assistance to them disguised as gifts.

But why? Is saving face so important?

Kalyani feels it is.

It is not that Paresh is entirely without self-respect. He has thought long and hard before deciding to ask Niren to not stay with them. And yet....

What is the point?

After he had slaved over a number of drafts for over an hour and finally managed to write a letter that preserved a façade for him while ensuring that Niren would not visit, Paresh had just put the pen down and called for Kalyani to come and hear what he had written when what should they hear at the front door but a voice he has heard a long time ago; 'Cousin! How are you? I hope you are at home!'

Paresh quickly slides the letter under the mattress and

smiles with an effort as he drags himself outside.

'Fancy seeing you here! You have arrived already? I was just about to write to you….'

As Niren counts his change and pays the porter who stands behind him, he laughs and says, 'What were you writing? "Brother, even though I am happy that you are coming, it is a fact that…and hence …"'

Paresh casts a quick eye at the shiny leather suitcase balanced atop the porter's head and the freshly laundered silk shirt that Niren is wearing before he laughs loudly and says, 'Why would I say that? I was being direct and saying – do not come here, we have no space. Your sister-in-law does not like outsiders to enter our love nest and so on…'

The way he says it, there could be no doubt that it is a joke.

Needless to say, Kalyani was also there. She pretended to be affronted and said, 'Listen to him! What false accusations against a lady!'

'You should sue him for defamation!' Niren entered the house and said, 'Where are the children? How come I cannot see any of them?'

'They have gone out to play, they will be back very soon. So, what has been happening with you?'

'As if you have lost sleep over how we have been! Thank God I came here….'

'As if you would come if your work had not brought you here….'

'Fine, let us stop with arguments! Can you give me a cup of tea?'

Tea! A cup of tea!

What does it feel like to fall from the skies?

What cup is Kalyani going to use to serve tea to this man with a diamond ring on his finger, a silk shirt and a fine dhoti from Farashdanga? The three cheap cups that they do have at home are all missing handles and saucers.

Why did he boorishly need to come so soon and not give them time to prepare for his visit?

The children would be home any minute. What was Shontu wearing? The blue striped half shirt? The shirt which had lost its collar ages ago? Meenu was wearing a frock made from cutting down one of Kalyani's old voile sarees.

She could ask her neighbour Latika for one of her marble look cups, but what about the children's clothes and shoes? What of her own drab faded sarees?

They say thoughts are faster than the wind. Kalyani thought of so many things in the blink of an eye but so many things were left untouched. The owner of the diamond ring stayed.

New pitfalls presented themselves at every turn, bringing new worries with them.

Every step was accompanied by such shame.

Niren does not show off but even his normal ways are like showing off in Paresh's eyes. The ingredients that

Paresh brings home in exchange for his blood, sweat and tears; the preparations that Kalyani serves Niren, despite the grind of daily life – how easily their guest pushes that to the side of his plate. He eats half a sweetmeat and drops the rest into the glass of water he has been drinking from without hesitating.

Paresh had to see this happen three days out of the four that their guest has been with them. Unable to put up with it any more, he finally snapped this morning and said, 'Why throw it away? Can the children not eat their uncle's leftovers?'

Niren gives them a long lecture on the ills of eating food off someone else's plate.

But to save face in front of Niren, the children have been given goodies as well, but that is like 'pouring drops of water on hot sand' as the saying goes. Besides, who throws away food bought with good money?

Who would have thought that sweets could be discarded for being too cloyingly sweet?

At least the savouries were made by Kalyani herself; but they were thrown into the rubbish because as Niren observed, 'They all seem to have been fried in vegetable shortening!'

Whatever it was, Niren thought everything in Calcutta was impure as he had come from the western part of India. He did rue having to throw things away, but that was more annoyance with the corruption in Calcuttan society. He did not regret being denied the food or the fact that he had wasted it.

Four days passed but it felt like four years. He was apparently going to stay for six more days. It was only the twenty sixth and to top it all, this month was thirty one days long.

The polite, sociable Kalyani, the one who wished to preserve face just came and gave a shopping list to Paresh. Had she written all the names she could think of or had she lost her mind completely?

It was not even the end of the rainy season, and she was asking for cauliflower and peas. Why not young green jackfruit and Moringa drumsticks as well? Meat, eggs, cauliflower, peas, large carp fish, a lot of large prawns, gourd and coconuts, raisins and prunes – what a long list!

These will not be available in the local markets but they could be brought from Calcutta by sending someone. The neighbour's servant would do it if he was given something extra. Along with some sweet yogurt and clotted rabri.

'What is all this?'

No matter how quiet he keeps his voice, his rage is palpable.

Alarmed, Kalyani asks, 'What?'

'I mean this list. Is this for my funeral feast?'

Kalyani raises her eyes in shock, at what she hears him say! He has never said anything this harsh in his life. She says miserably, 'We have fed him plain rice and fish for a few days, I thought of doing something special for a couple of meals before he leaves.'

'Plain fish and rice! I have to borrow money to keep him in fish and rice for these four days, do you know that? I feel sick when I think of that, I will not be able to borrow any more!'

Kalyani said tearfully, 'What of the toys he brought the children from Calcutta yesterday, the picture books he gave them? That alone would be worth more than you borrowed – '

'It could be even more, but how does that help me? Can I buy you cauliflower and peas in exchange for toys at the shops?'

The tears that Kalyani had held back now rolls down her cheeks.

What horrible words to use! Why does he not understand, these demands are not for her own happiness but to maintain face?

Isn't his honour being saved as well?

If Niren repays the cost of fish and rice with presents worth five times more, will Paresh be seen as a generous host? At least if the hospitality is without compare and the food is generous, there is a chance of salvaging some lost ground. Who knows whether he will give a few more presents before he leaves; what will Kalyani do then?

Who is Kalyani anyway? Niren is not from her side of the family, the honour is all Paresh's. But will he understand this simple logic? It is not good to have debts, but Niren is not going to visit them repeatedly. They may never have another chance of hosting him or repaying him for the presents he has given.

They may well have to go through even tougher times the following month but at least they can save face now.

But Paresh seems to have taken a stance like a wild horse. He cannot be convinced to spend any more money even after a lengthy argument. He will buy all the best ingredients but only if Kalyani can give him the money to spend; if she has anything saved up that is.

Alas! Does he not know all about what she has!

Does she have anything stashed away anywhere?

The little gold that she had was pawned when Shontu had typhoid the other year. Not a piece of foil is left over.

So Kalyani does something quite unusual in her state of angst.

She says, 'You go and borrow the money, I will repay it somehow later.'

'Really? Fine! Why don't you take a little more of everything, that way you will be able to send a box of sweets for his wife and children the day he leaves?'

Paresh takes the list and leaves for the market with a peculiarly cruel smile.

Niren comes home in a little while.

It was just as Kalyani had feared. He had bought a beautiful saree from Calcutta for her.

She protested, 'Why have you done this? No, never! I cannot accept such a costly gift! You spent all that money for no reason.'

It is not easy to say no to Niren. Instead of getting angry he keeps smiling as he says, 'For no reason? The true fulfillment of money is when it is spent adorning a woman. Suppose I was to get a pair of pants made for myself, do you think anyone would give me a second glance? But a saree, now that garners both my happiness as well as praise for the good taste I have. Tell me, I do have good taste, right?'

'You have very good taste! But you must give things to those that look good in them. Where will I ever go, and when will I ever wear this saree? Take this and give it to your wife.'

'As if I have never given her a saree!'

Kalyani smiles despite the turmoil within her. She replies, 'Of course you have! And long may you continue to give them to her!'

'That goes without saying. But why can I not give a saree to someone else if I wish to do so – I didn't know that was a rule?'

'No rule! But I really do not want to accept this saree. Perhaps, if you had bought something ordinary—.'

'No, that I don't want to do.'

'Your brother will be upset with me.'

'Really? Well give him two scoops of rice extra if he gets angry.'

Who can argue with such a man?

'I can't argue with you! You will not stop till I have accepted this, will you?'

'There! Finally you begin to understand what I am like!'

Kalyani showed Paresh the saree later that night. It was a Tangail with amulets on the border woven with golden thread.

She had assumed he would be angry, that she would have to plead with him to keep the saree but it turned out a little differently.

'Nice saree!' he said before turning on to his side and falling asleep. As if he felt that since Kalyani was so overwhelmed by the saree, there was nothing more to add.

At least he did not display his annoyance in front of Niren. The day actually passed in fun and laughter. He bought everything that Kalyani had asked for. They ate amid much laughter and chatter. They even go out in the evening to stroll about in the moonlight. Their outer suburban neighbourhood is pleasant at night even though there are quite a few factories.

Overwhelmed by all the new sights, Kalyani says, 'We have lived here for so long but I never knew that one could go out at night!'

'Amazing! Well my brother, this does not involve spending money. Why not do this once in a while?'

Niren teased Paresh about his 'miserly' nature at every opportunity. He explains away any shortcomings in their daily life as consequences of his brother's laziness and miserliness and laughs conspiratorially with Kalyani.

Paresh responds with equal humour.

But it was impossible to extract a smile out of Kalyani the day before Niren was due to leave. She seemed to have conceded defeat in a great battle. Every attempt by the loquacious Niren to amuse her fell on deaf ears.

Eventually Paresh had to say, 'You look like you will be the hardest hit by the coming separation!'

He was joking, of course, but was there an undercurrent of jealousy as well?

The value of a little humour and kindness in the midst of a hard monotonous life can be quite a lot. But surely that did not mean that she would exclude herself from all conversation while their guest was still there? This seemed like a little too much.

Something happened the next day to add to Kalyani's already heavy heart. Niren had hung up his silk shirt with its gold buttons on a rack in the courtyard a day or so earlier as was his habit; now when he went to put it on, he found the buttons missing.

But they did not have a servant to blame for the missing buttons. Then who could have taken them?

The buttons had particular sentimental value as they had been a wedding gift.

Paresh looked all over the house through the morning, turning everything upside down and checking every possible hiding place as well as the impossible ones. He took it as a personal slight that Niren had lost something of value while under his roof.

Kalyani goes about her work silently with a worried look on her sad face.

Niren did not assist in the search, choosing instead to sit and brood in silence. He seemed overly affected by the loss. It is as if he has lost something of far greater value than a few buttons. The loss is hardly going to make a difference to him financially.

Was it because they had been a wedding gift?

Eventually, Paresh, who had looked everywhere,decided to give up the search.

He sat down exhausted and exclaimed, 'They are to be found nowhere! Peculiar!'

'It is not peculiar at all!' Niren said somberly. 'I knew they would not turn up, you wasted your time looking.'

'What does that mean? I do not think I like the tone of your voice? Do you suspect someone?' Paresh sounded hurt.

'I do not suspect anyone. I am simply saying that when buttons go missing from a shirt, it is an utter waste of time to go looking for them behind trunks and underneath the beds.'

Paresh said angrily, 'Look Niren, just because we are poor does not mean we have no honour. What a lesson this is turning out to be!'

'It has been quite a learning process for me too, but accompanied by sadness. I suppose one must pay for experience. But please, do not make such a "show" of looking for the things!'

'Are you trying to say….'

'Me? I am not trying to say anything. Let us not discuss this any further, I am not enjoying this at all.'

Niren left the house without saying another word.

As soon as he had gone, Paresh came to the kitchen with a terrible expression on his face and said, 'Listen, I have to ask you something.'

'What do you mean?' Kalyani sounds very quiet.

'Where did the money you gave me yesterday come from?'

'I had it.'

'You had it? Pray tell, how did you manage to hold on to it for so long despite the gaping need of the household?'

'I had given it to Latika for safekeeping.'

'Kalyani! Look at me! Look up at me! Shame on you, when did you sink so low? Unimaginable! I was just saying to Niren that being poor does not make one dishonourable!'

Paresh keeps tugging at his own hair, his enraged face unrecognisable as the veins throb in his temples and his blood shot eyes glare at Kalyani.

'Do you think that I….?' Kalyani's pale lips tremble in anguish.

'Me? Oh, not just me! Even the person who has been

robbed, do you think he is not thinking the very same thing? Do you want to know what I feel like? Lord! I feel it would be best if I did not return alive from the factory today, that it would be best to give in to the sharp teeth of the machines or the fire in the boilers and end this shame!'

Paresh did not seem capable of controlling what he said. He said all the harsh bitter words that he knew to vent his disgust for Kalyani and then left hurriedly for the factory.

Paresh went but what of Niren? Did he not come back?

Of course, he did. One has to return in order to make preparations for leaving. There was one other reason for him to return. He could not suppress his wish to say a few words to mock Kalyani. Just a few words – about how she had not wished to accept his gift made in love on the grounds of self respect; but that same self respect had not prevented her from stooping low.

Are women always pretending to be something that they are not?

Kalyani, child-like and innocent as a young girl; at least that was what Niren had thought of her. But she had dispelled all his illusions. She had not even left him the scope to close his eyes to what had happened. There was little point in thinking that she was innocent, for a person that left proof of their wrongdoings lying about in the open and went about their day was more stupid than anything else.

Stupid Kalyani, who had the cunning to summon a goldsmith and sell the stolen gold but not the intelligence to hide the receipt? Why had she carefully kept the instrument of her downfall close at home like King Ravana of myth?

Of course, she had to be careful with it; the goldsmith had left it with her because the money had not been paid in full. It had come to light thanks to Paresh, and his zealous search for the buttons.

Niren fished the proof out of his pocket.

He planned on doing nothing more than showing it to her and asking, 'What is this?'

He wished to see what she said by way of explanation.

He came to the kitchen and stood at the door, prepared to unleash a battery of caustic words. Did he stand at the door or did he come to a halt?

But the words? Who robbed the normally vocal Niren of all the things he had been prepared to say? What made him incapable of even calling out to Kalyani, let alone harangue her?

Why does he stand silently outside the door and gaze transfixed at the person within the room? What does he see in her?

Shame? Injury? Fear?

Perhaps, but there are so many other things too.

Does Niren know how to read expressions? He must; why else would he stand silently for so long? Eventually he bows his head in respect.

Kalyani sits before the glowing furnace, only half her face visible from where Niren stands. What can be seen is a play of light and shadow. A little hint of sunken cheek, the hard line of her jaw, a single lowered eyelash, a rough wisp of hair curled about the temple – that is all.

Do they speak of the failures of Kalyani's existence? Of the death of her hopes? Do they tell the story of how helpless she is?

Has Niren managed to decipher the frozen silence of her story?

But then, what if he has? Isn't every civilised member of society helpless in that respect? Can Niren even tell her that he understands?

He leaves in silence, just as quietly as he had come to the kitchen, suitcase in hand. He does not feel like calling a porter this time.

'Did you hear what happened? Do you know what Niren said before leaving?'

Paresh talks loudly on his return from the factory. He said to Kalyani, 'Put everything aside and come and listen to this! The whims of rich people! He put the buttons in the inside pocket of his shirt and forgot all about them. Then he raises a fuss over stolen buttons! We have neither servant nor maid, who is going to steal things in this house? He is lucky I am a good-natured fellow, anyone else would have come to blows over such allegations! Of course, I cannot lie, he did ask for forgiveness many times. He even went and saw me at the factory before going to the station. I noticed that he was very contrite about expressing his suspicions earlier in the morning. He kept asking to be forgiven – of course, it was not really enough compared to what he did earlier.

Paresh kept talking, almost to himself. He did not seem to notice Kalyani's complete silence or perhaps he did not wish to notice it. Perhaps he wished to erase the harsh words that he had spoken to her earlier, by piling word on top of word.

If he had bothered, he would have seen – but then, what would he have seen?

Does everyone have the ability to see? Or to read the language that is spoken in silence.

Deathly Blow

(Mrityubaan)

It was almost ten o'clock by the time family and friends finished congratulating them. It was not a small group by any means, those who were frequent visitors had been joined by those who were hardly ever seen in that house.

It was inevitable that they would all come, for who could have a moment's peace without seeing Sunanda after the event? Sunanda has become an object of curiosity for everyone. Of course, they would probably not have descended on them all together, they would have come one at a time. As and when they found it convenient, in the morning or at night, in the afternoon, today, tomorrow or the day after in some cases. The credit for gathering them all here at once goes to Niranjan.

He invited everyone that could come to a tea party without telling Sunanda.

It is no laughing matter when a lost wife is found. How many are ever that lucky? And not just any old wife, but a wife like Sunanda; one who is without compare in beauty, brains, behaviour and conversation; why, just try and find another quite like her. Many people envy Niranjan because of Sunanda.

Sunanda was astonished when Niranjan came back at three o'clock with a few big boxes filled with cakes, sweets and biscuits.

'What is all this for?'

'People will eat all this.'

'What do you mean? Why will people come to your house to eat cake for no reason?'

Niranjan raised his face and looked at Sunanda, smiling a little as he said, 'Why not? This is the way to express happiness after all! Feeding people on cake.'

Sunanda seemed to melt with happiness and pleasure. She made a face as she spoke softly, 'An old worn out wife, nothing would change if she had been lost! You could have remarried, a more modern younger woman this time.'

'Remarry? All this again?'

Sunanda could not quite understand the tone of Niranjan's words, despite being very clever. She, therefore, laughed a little and said, 'As if you wouldn't! Would you have pined for me forever? What next!'

Niranjan kept opening the boxes and putting the food on the table. He said quietly, 'Even if I did want to remarry, where would I find a wife? What kind of wretch would give their daughter to another wretch who has already misplaced one wife?'

'What?' Sunanda seemed to dissolve in laughter. 'Did you lose your wife due to some sort of negligence? It was all due to her lack of sense. At the most, you could say that it was your misfortune. All the problems, the worries, the expenses – you are the one who had to bear the brunt of it all, did you not? If it was not your fate....'

'I am saying the same thing' Niranjan said as he crushed the used wrapping paper between his palms, 'it is my fault and no one else's, but what is the time now? Is it past three? Let me go and order the tea, there is no point waiting any longer.'

Sunanda widened her eyes and said, 'Tea on top of this? How much money do you want to spend? You have already spent so much!'

'This is for you too. How can I celebrate your return on my own? Should I not let everyone know?'

Sunanda frowned, 'Well, I understand that. But how will everyone know that you have got cake and sweets at home and are now going to get tea for them? Do they know how to read fortunes?'

'My will force will draw them all here,' Niranjan answered as he put his shoes on again.

Sunanda found proof of his will force from five o'clock in the afternoon.

It was like getting married all over again.

She had to wear a beautiful saree at his command, its red border matched by a red blouse. She wore a thick line of red vermilion in her hair parting and a huge red dot of the same on her forehead. These seemed to announce her good fortune to the world.

A new double dose of good fortune for the lucky Sunanda.

Just as many envy Niranjan for his wife, Sunanda too is envied by many women because of Niranjan's love for his wife.

She was greeting guests as she stood near the stairs, smiling continually, talking ceaselessly, it was as if five to seven years had disappeared in a trice.

Dear heavens! This was the wife that Niranjan had lost.

Everyone was thinking the same thing.

His cousin Basanti came up the stairs ponderously. She did not wait to catch her breath but spoke straight away, 'I must say, what a thing to do! Our brother nearly went mad!'

Sunanda smiled sweetly and said, 'Is that new? I have always had that effect on him!'

'Who can parry at words with you? But I had to tell your brother-in-law off!'

'Why? What did that gentleman do wrong?'

'What did he not do wrong? He has always said I am a stupid lump of a woman. He has always been full of praise for you! What happened this time? However stupid I might be, no one has stolen me away! No one could trick me like that!'

Her husband now followed his beloved 'lump' of a wife upstairs. Sunanda looked at him and smiled her usual little smile before saying, 'One would have to hire a truck to steal you away, how would they manage that quietly?'

'Listen to that! Are you satisfied now?' the husband laughs uproariously.

Basanti puffs even more with anger, 'Then an elephant like me is a far better wife to have! At least no one will come close for fear of having to pay for transport!'

Sunanda pinches her rubbery cheeks and laughs happily.

Another of Niranjan's cousins, Nitish, comes bounding up the stairs, 'So you are here all in one piece then?'

'Why would I not be?' Sunanda shakes her handkerchief at him prettily.

'Did your brother invite you to my funeral? Is that why you are surprised to see me here?'

'Not at all! But what a thing to happen! Whatever you say, I never thought this was something that could have happened to you. Like cheap tabloid news – "Sunanda X falls prey to conman." You behaved very foolishly. Did you not suspect anything? You just went with a stranger? You could not have waited till the servant returned, you simply left the doors open and....'

Sunanda said mysteriously, 'I did not think you would say such foolish things either! Did you believe that tabloid story as well?'

'What do you mean? Why would I not believe it? Was something left out of the story?'

Niranjan was coming back in a hurry, he had to pay the man who had brought the tea from the restaurant. He pushed past Nitish and went upstairs quickly and as he passed, Sunanda laughed loudly and said, 'Do you think I was really kidnapped by someone? I ran away myself, just cut the ties and ran away. I fell out of your brother's arms. Then, I remembered you all. I had to come back.'

'Lucky that you are all there then,' Niranjan said, as he ran downstairs with the money again.

Sunanda talks to each person in a different way. She sits by the older women, a picture of soft, gentle, serenity – her face shadowed by traces of her recent trauma.

The bright red border of her saree, the brilliance of her blouse, the vermilion in her parting do not bring ferocity to her appearance any more but rather impart a chaste look, desirable for all faithful wives.

How did she manage to mute the colour like that?

'I cannot begin to imagine that day, Aunt. He looked like a gentleman, he had a car with him – how was I to know he was a cheat? When he said, "I am coming from Medical College, if you come with me you will at least be able to see your husband before everything is over! He was in a motor accident, so I do not hold any great hope for his survival!" Just imagine my plight? My world seemed to spin around me and everything went dark.'

The aunt in question made soothing sounds.

Sunanda continues, 'My heart was trembling, my hands were shaking, my throat felt dry but I still managed to think of asking, "How did you know about this house? The man took a notebook out of his pocket and showed me the address written. It belonged to your nephew. He had lost it a few days ago, how had this man found it? He said it was in your nephew's pocket. It was all muddied and flattened. Tell me, how was I to control my feelings?'

The aunt agrees again, 'Absolutely, something as precious as a husband! How were you to keep calm? Still, I must say that you are very clever and brave to have managed to give that scoundrel the slip and escape with your honour unblemished! What did you do for the five days?'

'What did I do? God knows, dear Aunt! I do not know how I spent those five days. How did I go without ten meals?'

Tears pour freely from her enormous eyes.

'Sorry, sorry, God bless you!' a torrent of regret and sympathy flows through the room.

A curious little girl asks, 'Why did that man take you away Aunty?'

'Why do you think?' Sunanda pulls on the beribboned hair and says in a childish tone, 'Because he was a thief!

Can you not see, all my jewels are gone! My bangles, my necklace, the rings with the red stones – do you not remember? All gone!'

'Every-thing?' the child says in dismay, 'Didn't you cry?'

'Of course, I did! I cried so much that they had to let me go, if not they would probably have hacked me to pieces.'

'That would have been better!' a distant sister-in-law breathed heavily and said, 'Being killed would be better for a woman. We have so many things to worry about. On top of that, you are so beautiful. We are better off, we might look like blackened wood but still. So, did they beat you up to get the jewellery from you?'

She looked quite hopeful of hearing more stories of brutality.

A dark shadow of pain seems to descend on Sunanda's face. 'No, he did not touch me. I gave them myself. Thankfully, I had quite a bit of gold on me. The value of the gold would be a lot at today's prices. Once I gave him all that, I begged him to let me go. You are right my sister, the dark skinned old ones are not at risk.'

Her sister-in-law gave her an even darker look and took a large sweet from the plate.

Question after question – as she answers them, it becomes easier.

She might have lost her mind when the kidnapper came for her in the afternoon but she is now firmly standing on her own feet and she has the safety of numbers.

She will not lose her mind now, nor muddle her words. She laughs and makes sure everyone hears her as she says to Niranjan, 'If someone came and said to you, that I was in hospital with a cracked skull, would you have been able to think clearly? Would you remember to verify whether this was true or false? Would you be taking the time to lock doors or run to me as you were?'

Niranjan said, 'If I heard something had really happened, I would have gone to you. But why do you sound like I have blamed you for getting kidnapped?'

It was ten o'clock before everyone left and the last guest had been told farewell. Some more time passed before they could get to bed.

Sunanda was sitting on the bed when Niranjan came and sat on the chair.

She had not taken off the new saree or its blouse yet, the vermilion dot burned just as brightly. Does it not get smeared because she is fair skinned? So many women seem to wear just a little dot and soon even that is smeared all across the forehead and down their noses.

As she lies on the bed, she looks at the mirror. Truly, she looks so desirable tonight, the colour red has a really attractive quality about it.

She is the first one to talk.

'So many people! I am exhausted from talking so much! Why did you have to get all those people together tonight?'

Niranjan gets up to adjust the fan and sits down again.

'It was a good thing that I did. Everyone would have come anyway, right? I just got them all here on the one day; that way your story has been told and there are no discrepancies. If you had to say it again and again, you might make a mistake.'

'Mistake? Make a mistake with the story?'

Tears well in her eyes but she still smiles and says, 'Is it our wedding night today?'

Niranjan shifts a little and says, 'It looked a little like that, did it not?'

Sunanda covers her head and sits with her hands idle in her lap in a very demure fashion. She never covered her head in the bedroom and it made her face look very peaceful.

Niranjan does not say any more. He looks at her bright red dot. He cannot stand the wearing of these dots but she still wears them. Why does she do it? A little coloured dot! How it alters the face!

Just like a scratch of ink alters the world.

Had she not been wearing the dot in the middle of her unlined smooth forehead, what would she look like? What would the world look like if Niranjan did not have in his pocket a piece of paper with a few marks in ink, waiting like sleeping snakes?

'What are you looking at?' Sunanda smiles sweetly.

'Have you never seen me before?'

'Who knows? Perhaps not!'

'That is good then. Look at me more closely now, right? Now I am doubly precious, am I not? You probably had to spend a lot more than you did when we first got married.'

'I probably did. If you take the jewellery into account, it would be five to six thousand rupees.'

'Five to six thousand!'

Sunanda makes her huge eyes even bigger, 'You wasted so much money?'

'Wasted? Well, if you want to call it that. Of course, one must pay to have something one wants.'

'What a thing you got for all that money!' Sunanda purrs in an ecstatic voice, 'But what did you spend so much money on? Police? A detective? Lost and found advertisements? Transport? Did everyone trick you into handing over your money?'

'Of course, that is the rule. Just look at this letter alone! I paid fourteen hundred rupees for a letter that is only a few lines long.'

'A letter?'

Sunanda looks at him, astonished.

'Oh, did I not tell you? Here you go.' Niranjan fishes for a piece of paper in his pocket and holds it out.

'He had asked for eighteen hundred, I couldn't get him to agree to less than fourteen hundred.'

'What is this?'

A strangled scream issues from Sunanda's lips. She swoops like an eagle at Niranjan's hand and asks again, 'What is this?'

Niranjan has pulled his hand back just in time; a strange smile appears on his face as he asks, 'Can you not recognise this? Why? This is written clearly enough, you cannot recognise your own hand – that is unusual! Why, don't you think this is your handwriting? I could read it very clearly indeed.'

Niranjan holds two corners of the paper and tries to prove that he can read it.

Sunanda suddenly feels that the little letter is growing in Niranjan's hands, growing till it covers his face and then his hands; growing bigger till it covers the world and blots out her future.

Is this a piece of paper or an arrow with her name on it?

There is nowhere in the world where she may escape any more – the black inked letters crawl all over and threatens to blind her.

'Destroy that, you must tear that up!'

'Tear this up? What are you saying?' Niranjan's smile seems to grow cruel, every line and crease in his face smiling back at her.

'Who would tear up such a precious thing? Let it be, it is safe with me; this way there is no fear of anyone else in the world seeing it.'

He folds it carefully and puts it back in his pocket.

The same letter that Sunanda had written sitting in that same chair, to her childhood friend Kamalaksho. In which she had begged him to rescue the captive Sunanda from her cage. She had declared that she was unable to pretend any more, that she was tired, that she was ready to be rescued. She craved a little home filled with peace, just the two of them, away from prying eyes. She would sell her jewellery if that was the only way.

Kamalaksho had fulfilled her request partly of course; taking her jewellery for expenses. But when it came to making a home together, perhaps he thought two was a crowd and that was why Sunanda had found herself abandoned, in a waiting room in a provincial station.

'Even though you are tired – one must admit you are carrying on the pretence successfully. I congratulate you. You have maintained my social position and respectability through your intelligence….'

'And you? You will put away that letter – that poisoned arrow meant for me?' Sunanda screams.

'Poisoned arrow? That is a good description!' Niranjan laughs out aloud.

'You do know how to pick the right phrases! It must be because of all the novels you read! Poisoned arrow indeed, but I wonder who it was for', Niranjan smooths his pocket down as if to make sure that the letter is still there.

Love And Other Failings

(Shorshe O Bhuut)

Pratibha discovered a terrible truth as soon as she set foot in her father's home. It did not take her even twenty four hours to find this out.

Disaster! She has been gone for seven months and all this has happened in that time! Of course, it is not a real surprise given how simple her mother is. She only knows how to work herself to the bone all day, she never has an eye on what is happening around her. And her father has been a good-natured simpleton forever. If it was not for Pratibha, things would have gone pear shaped a long time ago.

Pratibha has actually been married for two years but she has never lived with her in-laws for more than two months at a stretch. She went with her three-month-old infant son this last time to live there permanently. That was six or seven months ago.

She came back because of dizzy spells and ill health.

She might be ill but she has not gone blind. Her eyes spotted the changes in her younger sister, Anubha's behaviour immediately.

This was nothing else but love!

Anubha had taken advantage of Pratibha's seven-month-long absence and decided to go and fall in love!

After dinner was over, Pratibha went and sat near her mother where the older woman was in the store room. Her mother had to be told.

Despite 'working herself to the bone', Shantilata still seemed to be keen to do more. She was preparing for the following day by chopping vegetables. She looked at her daughter and affectionately said, 'Come and sit down, I haven't had a good look at you since you came yesterday. Has your son gone to sleep?'

'Yes he has gone to sleep. But I see that you are all asleep as well!' Pratibha drew closer to her mother.

'Why do you say that?' the docile Shantilata looked fearfully at her aggressive and voluble daughter.

'Why? I really have to praise your complete lack of awareness! Have you looked at Ani lately?'

'Oh, Anu?' Shantilata sounded relieved. 'You must mean her marriage? What can we do, she wants to do a BA degree and she will not give up on that! I told her, she had passed two courses and that was enough, but she did not listen….'

'Did not listen? Great! She did not listen so the two of

you must heed her command. Amazing! You have obviously lost control over this daughter.'

'But lots of women are studying these days', Shantilata looks at her elder daughter with a little worry, aware of what she is saying this time.

'Why shouldn't they study? Let them study for all I care! I am not talking about that – but have you noticed her behaviour lately? Always distracted, no decorum in her words, she used to love the baby so much before, even that seems to have worn off. She shows affection only because she has to.'

'Are you mad?' Shantilata tries to defend her younger daughter. 'She was counting the days till your arrival with the baby.'

'That is all for show! I can see through all of that.'

Shantilata began to laugh on hearing this. She says, 'Is she not able to look after the baby for you as much because of her studies?'

'Don't be silly Mother! I am not talking about the baby! Will you not notice things unless I point them out to you? I am talking about that young man – that Debashis – why does he have to come here every day?'

'Debashis? You mean our Nebu? Anu is in the same college as his sister and so he helps her with her studies. He is such a good boy!'

Shantilata felt relieved when she finished. As if she had managed to quell her eldest daughter's worries.

But alas! Who can reassure the person who derives pleasure from battling with worries and apprehension?

Pratibha's beautifully formed mouth sags in disapproval – 'Such a good boy! I get so annoyed when I hear this sort of loose observation! And do such good boys not know how to "trick" girls into friendship? You will not even understand if I tell you things in a roundabout way, so there is no point in doing that. Helping her with her studies? That help is how this kind of thing starts! It is just an excuse for the two to spend two hours together chatting.'

'What are you saying? He talks about a lot of things with your father, he respects me so much as his "Aunt", how can you say such things about a boy like…' Shantilata protests.

'I am not accusing your boy of murder, am I?' Pratibha snarls.

'Those good boys are the ones who are more likely to fall in love! You would know if you had read a novel or two. Helping Ani with her studies, addressing you fondly, talking to our father about things – this is just how it all happens in the novels too. If you do not step in soon, you people will pay the price later on.'

'Okay, well you are here now, why do you not take the role of stepping in', her mother focuses her attention on the vegetables now. It is clear that not only does she not appreciate such keen scrutiny by her daughter; she also wishes to end the discussion here.

It is clear that she has great confidence in her younger daughter.

Well, fine then! What does Pratibha care? She has warned them of the consequences, she has done her duty. They will suffer if they are not careful.

'What is it to me? I am all taken up with my own health! I simply informed you because I thought you should know. The world is not as wet behind the ears as you people anyway!' Pratibha gets up and leaves in a huff.

The implication is that even if Shantilata is wet behind the ears, Pratibha is completely aware of all the evils of the world.

Pratibha did go to bed angry but was it possible to fall asleep so easily in that state? For those who forego sleep for the sake of everyone else's good, it is even harder. She stared closely at the bed next to hers before speaking up, 'Ani, haven't you slept yet?'

'No,' came the answer from the other bed.

This was in contrast to what used to happen in the past.

In the past, Anubha would sit up quickly on hearing her sister come to the room and ask whether her sister was thirsty, whether the baby needed his bottle, was it cold water from the jug or hot water from the thermos that she had to pour. They talked so much as well.

Instead, all she said was a short 'No', devoid of any grace. That meant she was silent despite knowing that her sister had not slept. She did not even wish to talk to Pratibha.

This was nothing but proof of her spending all her time thinking about the 'good boy'.

No! This was unbearable!

There was little point in getting angry with their mother and washing one's hands off the affair. Pratibha would have to take charge. It would not do to let her sister be ruined.

'If you are not asleep, why are you not talking to me?'

'What will I say? What if your baby wakes up?'

'Don't act like you are losing sleep over the baby! You must be pining for that boy', Pratibha gets straight to the point.

Anubha asks, astonished, 'Boy? What is that?'

'As if you do not know! Why, that Debashis or whatever his name is! You will not be able to fool me!'

'But I have not tried to fool you at all, my sister!'

'You are admitting it then?

'Admitting what?'

'That the boy is in love with you?'

A soft laugh issues from the other bed.

'How can I know what he feels? I can only speak for myself.'

'It is the same thing. Everyone knows that you cannot clap with one hand. So, how long has all this been going on for?'

There is another laugh. The answer comes immediately after, 'How do I give you an exact date? I would have written it all down if I had known there would be a quiz.'

No, this was a hopeless case.

How could she have become so shameless in such a short time? No sense of decorum at all! Pratibha was a full four years older than her and she still spoke with such casual disregard? Pratibha feels really ashamed for her.

'Capital! There is not much left for you to learn then! On a trajectory to ruin! Do you not feel ashamed to talk like this?' Pratibha chides Anubha bitterly.

'Shame? Let me see', after a moment's silence Anubha says, 'No, none at all'.

'Oh, that I should live to see this! But why should you not behave like this? The indulgence you are given! As if you will sprout a pair of limbs from going to college! What a great example you are!'

Thwarted, Pratibha picks up the fan from the bed near her son's head and fans herself rapidly.

'Sister?' Anubha calls.

Pratibha does not reply.

'Was your husband meant to come today?'

'Why? What does that mean? Who said that?'

'No one said anything. I guessed, looking at your mental state.'

Furious, Pratibha does not bother replying. Let her husband Shyamal come; she will decide on the next course of action after talking to him.

Shyamal comes the very next day.

He has been without his wife for all of sixty two hours, he just had to see her once. He could not say much that was critical of her parents, but still – he was not happy about their behavior at all. Should they not have invited him tonight to sooth his separation anxiety? They were very old fashioned and dull. His friends on the other hand had all been blessed with the most modern in-laws imaginable. They were far more liberal towards their daughters' spouses while also not neglecting their comfort.

As soon as he arrived, Pratibha blurted out her discovery in her opening sentences.

'You will never guess what happened!'

'What happened? You tossed and turned all night because you were thinking about me?'

'Whatever! Why would I think about you? No, it is something else – in the few months that I have not been here, Ani has gone and fallen in love with a fellow!'

'Only one?' Shyamal laughs loudly. 'That is alright then. It would be worrying if it were more than one!'

'You are always joking! Who knows what caste he belongs to....'

'Well, who else has the sort of talent you have my dear? To match all that caste and horoscope stuff, find an auspicious day and then say your wedding vows with the sacred fires as witness before falling in love.'

'You jest again? Stop it, I tell you – can these things be allowed to continue?'

'Who can stem the torrent of love with a wall of sand, my Beloved?'

'Stop your poetry! I say, we must get rid of this boy!'

'What? From the face of the earth?'

'No! But do you want Ani to get into a mess and your family to hear of such goings on? What if they cast aspersions when that happens?'

'Of course! But families have always been the judges of what is shameful.'

'Fine! Families are all bad then! But don't think that I will let this go just because she is my sister.'

'Are you mad? I think you should cast as many aspersions as you can!' Shyamal leans back in his chair as he speaks.

'You think everything is funny! But think about it, if your sister was doing this with someone, what would you do?'

'Then? Then, I would get a hunter and flay him alive!' Shyamal sits up this time.

'Of course! You would too! And yet, when it comes to my sister ....'

'Madre Dios! Sorry, My God! My own sister and your sister? That would be like comparing heaven and earth, the sky with hell!'

'But will we not say anything despite seeing a young unmarried woman giving herself away in such a tawdry fashion!'

'What is the harm? It is lucky she is unmarried, she has no one to answer to. One must do all the falling in love while they are this way, do you not agree?'

'The way you talk makes my skin burn! What if I had done something similar before we….' Pratibha made a peculiar face as she uttered the words.

'Hey! If only!' Shyamal lowered his cigarette and let out a puff of smoke before saying, 'There is no what if about that! I already know that you must have smitten a few swains before yielding to me!'

'I won't stand for that sort of talk, what kind of girl do you think I was?'

'That kind of girl? What are you saying? Love is one of the greatest virtues of civilisation. Do you wish to tell me that you did not cast a meaningful loving look at a single man before you met me, dear Pratibha?'

'Never! I am not like Ani!'

'Then I will have to say', Shyamal takes another long draw at the cigarette and says, 'That the Creator bestowed all this beauty on a most undeserving person! Anubha might have lost to you in the measure of beauty but she has more brains than her sister. She does not go about imagining the world to be Shankaracharya's monastery.'

'Then you want to tell me that Ani is doing a great thing?'

'Not a great thing, but she is doing what is normal. But who is the lucky fellow? Not me I dare say?'

'Do not toy with these things. Why, are you not satisfied with owning my affections completely?'

'No, not that at all – but my suspicions are a little aroused by the jealousy you show!'

'Jealousy? What a thing to say! Are there no morals left in the world anymore?'

'Of course, there are. They will continue to be there too. How else will you pass your time without them?'

Pratibha gets up and walks off in anger.

No, it was a mistake to involve Shyamal; what does he care! After all, the proverb did say that sons-in-law were never really yours. He would rather laugh slyly if some scandal was to befall his in-laws. But Pratibha was not going to be like that. She would have to do whatever she could on her own. If she didn't, then a handsome youth would be at their house everyday chattering with Anubha on the pretext of helping with her studies and she would grow more shameless each day; and that was not something Pratibha wished to see.

What else could be done? She had to be on guard constantly.

It was not like being at home where she had lots of chores to do. Here there was unlimited free time. She would spend some of that in the quelling of misdemeanors.

From that day on – when Debashis arrived, the one to appear in the study room was not Anubha but Pratibha.

'Hello, I was thinking of you!'

Debashis smiles as if he is a little embarrassed and uncertain about why he is being favoured so greatly and

Pratibha gushes, 'Today I will not let you go without having some tea, yesterday you left without having any!'

'But, I am not used to drinking tea at this time of day.'

'So what? Have some to make your sister happy', Pratibha raises her eyes at him; 'Although you are probably old enough to be my elder brother, but I am more senior in position. What do you say? Don't you agree?'

Even though she mentions the tea, she does not move from the chair. Anubha brings a cup of tea and puts it on the table with a clatter before leaving. Debashis tries to sound casual and succeeds in making his voice sound even more dejected as he asks, 'Don't you want help with that mathematical sum from the other day? You do not seem to be studying any more.....'

'Not today, I have a headache', comes Anubha's voice from outside. Pratibha feels like her stomach will burst with laughter. Good riddance! She has hit on the right plan! Just wait, Pratibha will fix all her symptoms of love.

But there is no point getting Debu angry. He is a son from a good family after all, an outsider too, it won't look good if she is not polite with him. And so Pratibha, despite hating poetry has to say, 'Anubha and studies! She is full of whims! Why do you not recite that poem by Rabindranath Tagore? You do it so well!'

'Another day, sister.'

'Okay then, if you do not want to. I had really enjoyed your recitation the other day.'

What is the poor boy to do then but read? What else can he do? He is a gentleman's son, an outsider, it does not look good if he is impolite either.

This problem fixing phase has been going on for a while.

As soon as she hears Debu, poor Pratibha has to drop everything and come rushing. Then it starts:

'Debu, why did you not come yesterday? I waited till nine for you to visit us', or 'Debu, do you remember that we have a date tomorrow? Let us go and shop for clothes, you have such good taste!....Are you talking about him? He is the most blind of people with no taste whatsoever!' or 'Debu, see how much the baby loves you? You must have been related to each other in a past life!'.... 'Now Debu, what a miser you are! Can you not ask me to go and see a film once?'.... 'Debu, did you not say there was a really good snack shop in your area? I tell you, I cannot eat a thing these days, as shameful as it sounds!'

It was like the coils of a snake. Where was Anubha supposed to fit herself in this situation?

But she had found a new way to amuse herself as well.

Whenever Shyamal visits these days, Anubha greets him instead of Pratibha with 'You just missed your wife! Who did she go out with? Why, our tutor?....'

'Come sir, let us wait for a couple of hours for them to be back.'

'Alas sir! You came so late, she was here all day today. Where? To the movies of course!'

'You are a lucky man today! She is at home. Not here though, up on the roof learning to play the sitar; did you not know? Not by herself, our tutor is a good sitar player too!'

'Won't you see your son before you leave? At least have a cup of tea. Nothing fixes heartache better. Will anyone else have a cup? No, it is just the two of us. We have the same affliction, do we not?'

Core Of Steel

(Ishpaater Paat)

It is a matter of wonder that both a bird and a tiger can be enclosed in a cage.

Bechulal swore under his breath and said, 'Evil speaks the same language everywhere.'

A dim light burned inside the room. The broad stripes of the saree wound tightly around Sukhi's soft curves looked like the markings of a tiger caged at the zoo from the other side of the bars.

At least to Bechulal who was slinking about like a ghost in the darkness behind his own house.

Who had ever seen a tiger outside a zoo anyway; Bechulal said to himself, 'At least the tigers in the zoo sit down occasionally.'

But tiger striped Sukhi was never still, spinning from

one side to the other, twisting her body this way and that. She was in the throes of passion.

Bechulal ground his teeth and then bared them in a rictus of hellish delight.

He said to himself again, 'The evil speak the same language everywhere!'

It was not clear who the bird was, who the tiger was and who sided with evil in this instance. But Bechulal looked a lot like a captive tiger as he wandered around the corners of his own house.

The silver disc at his throat caught a bit of a light every now and then and glimmered and the veins in his temples throbbed.

He stopped in one spot, stamped his foot and hissed, 'Tomorrow I will buy a whole chicken, just as fluffy and soft of flesh as Sukhi. I will prepare it with hot chillies.'

As he thought of this, the images of the chicken he would butcher and Sukhi kept mingling in his head.

Sukhi used to look like a bird before. Scrawny necked, thin. She would flutter at Bechulal's feet and protest, 'I cannot do that!'

Bechulal would pull her by her wings and say harshly, 'What do you mean you cannot do that? You will do that before you do anything else!'

'Did you not marry me and make me your wife?'

Bechulal would show his yellow teeth and cackle uproariously, 'But that is why I own you! I am your best teacher, understood? You must do everything I ask!'

'But to ask me to do this?'

Bechulal would slap her around the head and shoulders affectionately and say, 'Why not? You are not doing anything more than demeaning some evil people and getting money out of them. They don't think of you as any more than a street whore, they wrinkle their noses at people like us when they see us, as if they had seen a dog with sores. And now? Take that lady on the third floor of the house in front of us. The one who frets all night on an empty bed and struts about proudly during the day; the one who rides a car to do her daily shopping, her face sleek enough for a fly to slip off if it tries to sit on her? Try and sit next to her one day? She will shoot you down. But the man she frets for, you can have him at your beck and call. Isn't that a great thing?'

Bechulal would grow breathless as he said all this.

Sukhi never found anything to feel happy about in all this. Sukhi would say, 'But you want to cut off your own nose to spite someone else? You want to eat off the floor because a thief took your plates? Just because the rich look down on us means that you must invite them to our....'

Sukhi would cry out, 'Those are all excuses! You want your pretty wife to sell herself for you! Well, I just won't! I won't!'

Bechulal would take out his knife, with its blade as shiny as the midday sun and look at it.

'If you will not then this....' he would say, accompanying this with a cruel movement, like burying the knife to its hilt in soft flesh.

'Well, do that then!' Sukhi spoke without fear. 'Cut me into pieces with that knife of yours and cook yourself some dinner.'

Bechulal did not have a vestige of compassion in him. He smiled shamelessly and said with a cruel smirk, 'Why eat you in a day? When I can eat off you, if I keep you alive longer?'

'I married you with the gods as my witness, how can you make me do something so wrong?'

'Right? Wrong?' Bechulal laughed aloud as he said, 'Right and wrong, sins and good deeds – these are all mere words used by the rich devils. There is nothing in all of that. If you call a drink water, it is water; if you think of it as wine, wine it is. All words! Look at me. Don't I go to other women despite having a marriage witnessed by the gods? If I had money I would go more often. Do you like eating the same dish every day? Do you like the same fish with every meal?'

Sukhi went all quiet at that.

She got up suddenly from the floor. She twisted her clothing around a finger and said, 'Alright then, whatever you wish.'

'Great! Finally you are being a good girl!'

Bechulal could not help but marvel at his own

persuasiveness, at the beauty of his arguments.

He had not hoped to be this successful with his words; he had trusted the sunshine sparkling off his knife more. He would use fear to rid her of her concerns.

What was any other fear compared to the fear for one's own life?

The fear of doing wrong? The fear of sinning? The fear of what people might say? Nothing to it at all!

But his words were enough.

Sukhi picked her nails and said, 'But not from today.'

That meant she would, from the next day.

That meant opening the door to all kinds of possibilities.

The gentleman in the three storey house in front of their room had been pestering Bechulal for some time. He had wanted to pay him a lot of money.

He had not known that the woman who had caught his eye out of all the women getting water at the communal tap was Bechulal's own wife.

A fire had flickered up in the corners of Bechulal's eyes when he first heard the man's proposal. The knife he kept at home seemed to be begging to be brought out. But the fire changed colour slowly and turned into the colour of profit.

He had found a new way out.

He began to dream of foreign liquor. He began to dream of lying in bed till late, smoking his cigarettes rather than go out at dawn with his tools.

Bechulal thought, 'What a fool I have been! I have been starving when I have had a granary full of gold at home! Shame on me!'

The three storey houses that he had once felt like kicking down now seemed to amuse him. The thought that his wife would be taking something away from those superior women in their superior houses made him want to dance with happiness and the men he had once wished to beat senseless were once again objects of reverence.

He had to revere them of course.

THE story had picked up from there.

From three storeys to higher, and then lower and lower.

Bechulal was their guide.

Bechulal knew how to show them the way to hell.

This had made his dreams come true. Instead of looking for work in the mornings, he now spent those hours looking at fish and meat at the markets and deciding on what to have for lunch.

He was now able to taste the imported stuff regularly, in every sense of the word.

The whole day was spent in pleasure.

The only hassle was that he had to lurk in the vicinity of his own room, locked out at night with his knife always at the ready.

Yes, he kept the knife with him. Sometimes when he felt

the strongest desire to bury it in a particular soft body, slashing at the soft darkness that wrapped about him seemed to help.

At the start, it was not as painful.

The visitor quietly left his third floor home like a thief and tucked money into Bechulal's palm.

Sukhi had not learned to wrap the saree about herself so tightly and Bechulal had never thought of comparing the bars of a bird cage to those of a tiger's cage.

Bechulal used to laugh as he tipped out the bag filled with fish and vegetables and say, 'Make something good! You are working so hard you need to eat well too.'

Sukhi would put the things away with a glum face and say, 'You eat!'

'So, you are still brooding over all this? Get over it! Get over it! You are mine as you always were, it is just that the household is better run this way, don't you see?'

'Yes, I see,' Sukhi said as she disappeared into the other room.

But now the winds have changed.

Now Sukhi has learned to wrap a striped saree tightly about herself, she has learned to wear sandals on her feet and she has learned to treat Bechulal with disdain. She has learned a lot of things.

'The bird is now a tiger -'

Bechulal hisses his thoughts aloud; 'Now the tiger has tasted blood!'

She hides the money she makes. She gives him money

as though to a beggar. She also says, 'Only the gods know how a man can spend his entire life at home. Why does not something happen to him?'

Bechulal has to put up with all of this now. But today he is really angry. The reason is Sukhi's unrestrained laughter in front of the client with the car as she said, 'Do you know who this man is? This is my own husband!'

Why did she have to say that?

Did she not see how Bechulal was brought to his knees with that?

The client had suddenly decided, 'Come, let us go for a spin in the park.'

She could have just gone quietly, in her fancy sandals and her gaudy saree. Bechulal had not said a thing even though it stung him like fire. Why did she have to say so condescendingly, 'Come, you can come for a ride too! Just make sure you lock the door.'

The client was looking at them in amazement. She then had to add with a big smile, 'Are you annoyed? Let him stay at home then. Do you know who this man is? He is my lawfully wedded husband. It makes me sad that he has never had the good fortune of taking a spin in the park.'

Then she slammed the door shut and went off.

Was Bechulal going to sit in that car anyway?

But he has been simmering since then.

He will do something today.

'You are mine, nothing changes that', these words do not seem to affect Sukhi anymore. So, neglecting her will not work. That used to work at the beginning.

'Now the only way to teach her is with this', his blade gleams in the dark, bright as the sun.

A long time later, there came the sound of a car door being shut. In the next room, Latika whispered to her de facto Nondo and said, 'Have you seen how big Sukhi has become?'

'Of course I have', Nondo replied, 'This is why they say you should never trust women.'

'As if! Not all women are the same. Look at us, we are not paragons of virtue. But we are nowhere near her!' Latika said crossly.

Nondo did not answer her.

He was probably asleep.

But Bechulal does not go eavesdropping at these walls. He goes into his room and asks harshly, 'Are you asleep?'

Sukhi does not sit up suddenly at the sight of her husband like the other times. She yawns and says, 'I will go to sleep now.'

'I do not care whether you sleep or die. First give me all the money you just got paid. If you keep one coin from me I will kill you I swear.'

Sukhi sits up this time.

She cruelly taunts him, 'Really? But why?'

'You are questioning me? You have grown far too big for your boots!'

Bechulal bares the knife he had hidden in his pocket and says, 'Have you forgotten this?'

Sukhi pours more scorn into her voice and said, 'Why would I forget? How does one forget such a thing? In fact, I have had its twin made, just so that I do not forget it! Here, look…' Sukhi giggles.

She reaches under the mattress and fishes out the twin, holding her hand high just like Bechulal.

The dim light of late night is dispelled by a flash of sunlight.

Bechulal's blade has begun to rust at the handle but hers is shining from end to end.

Who knew that Sukhi had been gathering a steely determination a little at a time?

Stairways

(Sheenri)

This happened about ten years ago. We had no inkling that the storm clouds of the Second World War were already gathering in some corner of the skies above our world. We lived in complete peace. We had no idea that it would become illegal to buy rice at a rice shop or clothes from a clothes store. We only knew that 'tiger's milk could be bought if one had enough to offer', we had not yet had the fortune of finding out that a day would come when even basic medicines would not be easily available. Even if the gods themselves had told us that all the wealth of ordinary people would go up in smoke with the bombs of war, we would not have believed them. I doubt that even the most imaginative among us had any idea that one day, all that the people across the country would be left with was the clothes they were wearing.

In certain privileged parts of society, there was a certain luxury of agonising over 'our subjugated status' but it did not matter to clever people like us. When I walked into the house at the start of the month with my paycheck, I did not feel very different from an emperor ruling over the world.

On one such day, something happened.

Pesadi and her mother came to us in tears.

They were from our village and years ago, their ancestors had been 'perjas' or tenants of my landholder predecessors. Who else would she appeal to but us when circumstances forced her to come to Calcutta to find a way to survive? The horde of relatives that I had in the country home, a bunch of lice-idden individuals with enlarged spleens – had provided her with my address and she had then gone through a lot of trouble to find us – she gave a detailed description of that as she fell at my young wife's feet and entreated, 'You must give us shelter sister, or I will not move from here with this useless daughter of mine.'

I already said that this all happened ten years ago. Youth had not left my wife's body, nor compassion her heart and she did not think of pity, civility, good manners as laughable insanity. Therefore she spoke with heartfelt kindness and said, 'Let it be! Truly, where else would you go if not to us? Why don't you give a biscuit and some 'nyabenchush' lozenges to the girl, son? Her face looks quite pale. Do you want water to drink Pesadi?'

Pesadi agreed eagerly and after eating a fistful of biscuits and 'nyabenchushes' and drinking a gallon of water she revived a little. She then stared adoringly at her newly acquired aunt and said, 'Orey baas! She is like an idol! Like a white woman!'

Needless to say, Pesadi's mother stayed.

I cannot lie – the woman was not ungrateful. The maids of Calcutta would not be able to imagine working so selflessly for an employer; and with such a overwhelming sense of gratitude. To see what was given to her in exchange for her hard work as largesse and be grateful for that – only simple rural folk like these are capable of such gratitude. Sometimes my wife used to say, 'Why are you so worried about everything all the time, Pesadi's mother? Do you think the fellow we had previously did not need food or clothes, or did not get paid? He got everything and still shirked his duties.'

Pesadi's mother would reply pitiably, 'Do not say that sister! If I did not get shelter from you, where would I have found a place to try and settle down in this vast city? This is not a city I tell you, but an ogre's palace! It frightens me just to look at its streets. Where would I have taken my child? People would have driven her away. You are so compassionate. You give me tea twice a day, snacks to eat, hair oil – who does this much?'

Actually the girl did a lot as well. She was a skinny eight-year- old who would have done little more than whine all day if she had been born in more privileged surroundings. But Pesadi did one thing or the other all day long. I do not know where she found the time but somehow hanging out the washed clothes, making the beds, making tea and a lot of other chores became part of Pesadi's duties.

Our son became quite the little prince with someone to carry out his orders.

Sometimes I would say, 'You are ordering her around all day, what did you do before they came to us:? All I hear is "Pesadi, Pesadi!" Why?'

He would carelessly answer, 'She loves doing something all the time. Why does she come and keep asking me what she can do so often?'

I do not know whether our son was actually older than the girl but she was so conscious of her inferior situation that when she referred to him as elder brother, it did not feel amusing any longer.

And yet?

All of this happened about ten years ago. Years passed as years do. In the same way that we do not sense the daily rotation of the earth, we do not notice changes in our daily circumstances. I had not noticed that Pesadi had grown out of skirts and into sarees, that she did not follow us as closely as a puppy anymore and that she did not babble away non-stop the whole day as she had once done. Do you know when I noticed all that? It was when the war called for our evacuation.

When I was struggling like a patient with hydrophobia

to find a shelter which was not at risk of being bombed and pleading with both family and strangers, as well as people I had known for moments and those I had known forever, one day my wife opened up to me about the fears she had and said, 'I do not know where we will find a place to hide. I can go anywhere with a boy, but what of Pesadi? The girl has grown so much, she is tall enough to look like she is sixteen already – where will we go with her? If she was our own flesh and blood, it would have been different but this is a maid's child! Just because we think of them as family does not mean that others will as well'.

I saw the logic in what she said.

It was something to worry about. But a sense of humanity told me that we would not leave them behind when it was time. We could not forsake them in the hour of need. And yet, it did not seem that it was going to be easy. Even if I did push my wife and son into someone else's household like weeds in an established garden, I just could not fit the maid and her daughter into the equation. Relatives acted like enemies as soon as they heard my proposal.

Finally when I did manage to make arrangements with great difficulty, I found that I did not have to worry for Pesadi's mother any more, as she had made her own arrangements. A gentleman in a neighbouring house had sent his family off to his village and was living an orphaned existence at home – Pesadi's mother was going to provide a solution to his lack of cooking skills in exchange for a roof over her head.

As part of the responsibility I felt towards her, I thought it best to caution her one day, 'It is hard to know people in this city, what their real agendas may be – I just hope you do not find yourself in trouble once we are no longer here to provide you with refuge'.

She smiled and waved away all my baseless concern by saying, 'Do not worry about all that brother, the gentleman in that house is a man of great honour.'

I do not know when she had managed to find out about his honourable nature.

But since it was clearly not my concern anymore, I went with wife and son on a bone chillingly cold evening to deposit wife and child in a remote village filled with snakes, jackals and empty spaces and then returned to take up residence in a mess hall.

Even though the house was my own it was not possible to live in that large house by myself, was it?

An account of what happened next is unnecessary.

Every householder would remember how confused they were by the variety of information that they gathered from newspaper reports, government bulletins, false rumours and the realities of war. After risking life and limb to stay alive, after realising that it was best to die together with the family than die alone, when I could finally bring my family back to the city and begin living in familiar surroundings, the abandoned and neglected city began to come back to life again and a flood of humanity entered it like a river swollen by floods.

There were more unfamiliar faces than known families in our neighbourhood.

'Go to Anongo Babu's house and inform Pesadi's mother that we have returned', my wife said to me before she began unpacking our belongings. She was possibly hoping for help. It was not easy to return after being away for a year and half and make a broken household right again. When I expressed my doubt as to whether she would come straight away, my wife said, 'Why are you saying she will not come? She cried so much when we had to leave.'

But Pesadi's mother could not be found.

I heard that Pesadi's mother had left to work with one of Anongo Babu's nephews, immediately after his family returned to Calcutta.

There was nothing to be done but express regret over her loss.

Our absence was the reason the hapless woman had disappeared forever.

On the home front, the lack of domestic help was driving us around the bend.

Every evening my wife would list the numerous tasks she had to do that day and then praise Pesadi's mother's various qualities. She always said with great regret at the end, 'If only we had her address!' Her facial expression indicated her belief that I just was not looking for Pesadi in the right places.

But where was I to look for them in this huge city?

Even the gods are said to have granted appearances

after ardent prayers, so it was hardly a surprise that Pesadi's mother turned up eventually.

As soon I came home that evening my wife said, 'Pesadi's mother came to see me today.'

'She came here? What? The gods have looked up at last! Well, I hope you promised her a fairly big increase in pay? The old rates have changed.'

'Do you think of nothing but your own comfort? I can only think of paying her if she works here! She does not sweep floors for a living any more. She does not even work as a cook; she only does housekeeping these days. You will be amazed if I tell you how cushy her job is. How well she was dressed! A snow white chemise, a fine flower bordered saree, and Pesadi? She is better than the girls we see going to school. A printed blouse, a striped saree, arms covered in glass bangles and get this, she wore heeled sandals – that same Pesadi we once knew! She does not even talk the same way anymore. I also heard that the gentleman in the house they live in is paying for her to go to school and to have voice training. Apparently her voice is so sweet that she will be a radio artiste any one of these days.'

I was astonished.

Only the tumult of war could be held responsible for such a turn in their fortunes.

But even this happened a long time ago.

A lot of tumult happened in our lives as well. Our son did not turn out the way we had hoped. The two years of schooling he lost made him perform poorly. After pretending to study hard at home for a few days he gave up completely. Tutors did not help either. He has already started looking for shortcuts to success at this young age.

His mother is not very well these days and I have lately been made redundant at work.

But I digress, this is not my story after all.

This is the story of Pesadi and her mother.

Now we come to the present time.

No work has meant I am able to sleep for quite a while each day after lunch. Today I woke suddenly to familiar voices. A peep through the window showed me that my guess had been correct. The mother and daughter were sitting in the courtyard, in the same spot where Pesadi's mother had once collapsed at our feet in tears.

She wore a thick flattened beecha haar around her neck, a saree with a narrow black border and a long sleeved blouse in white. There is little need to describe what her daughter was wearing. I noticed, however, that the handbag Pesadi carried was quite expensive.

Pesadi's mother was obviously replying to something my wife had said earlier; I heard her say, 'I am so sorry to hear that you are in such dire straits. Tell my brother to come to me once, perhaps I may be able to help him. Everyone in the 'chinema' world respects my Mandalika, she has the manager's ear. Have you not seen her name and her photo in all the papers? What are you saying? You do not watch 'chinemas' at all? How can that be? Well, I will arrange for passes for you, go and have a look some day. What is the name of your new film, Pesa – sorry, Mandalika?'

Mandalika rubbed her powdered handkerchief into her neck and answered, 'Go into Battle.'

'Yes, that one! I cannot remember such long names. She took me to where they were 'chooting' one day. What a wonderful house it was! And to see how people looked up to her, she is a 'hiroine' you know! She just needs to say the word to her manager and she can get jobs for as many as five people! You were saying that your son did not manage to do anything with his life, perhaps he could sell tickets like he wants to. What is all this? No, no tea for·me at this time; no sweets either! I have got such bad reflux! Who? Mandalika? I wish! She does not touch sweets, ever since her teacher said they will ruin her voice. Tea? No she does not drink just any old tea; she must have the best kind. You did all this for nothing! Well, we will see you later then, a car is about to come from the 'chudio' to pick her up. Tell my brother we came, I say Mandalika, have you given the address for our apartment to her? I feel so bad you are in such a plight, after all you are from my own village.'

I think my wife was also as dumbstruck as I was – why else did I not hear her say a single thing?

Meaningless

(Orthoheen)

I was amazed to see them sitting side by side at the cinemas. It is amazing how people love spreading rumours.

Even though I could only see them from the back, I could hardly have made a mistake. I have lived for four or five years in the same house as them.

It would be close to ten years ago now that this newly-married, rather inexperienced couple came and set up house in the two rooms on the floor below us. The rooms were let out, not because we needed the rent but more because they needed the space. They had somehow come to know by virtue of a friendship with my nephew Binu that the two rooms we had downstairs which were closed to the south did not get used much. The man came and entreated us, he had found a wife for himself but no house and the situation was rather grim.

A situation that is quite common among those who choose their partners for love in our society. Neither family seems to give them the affection or the respect that they deserve. So they must hunt for a place in order to make a home together and preserve self-respect.

Were the rooms closed off to the south? For them, that was more than enough. It was heaven for them. Between the two they had all the southerly breezes they wanted.

But Anubha used to stay downstairs as little as possible, only while Amalesh was at home. She used to escape upstairs. Sometimes with some chore that she was doing, a piece of needlework, a bit of knitting, vegetables she was cutting up or rice she was sifting through.

She used to say, 'I am frightened of being on my own'.

But I knew that it was really our beautifully arranged home that drew her. She had a great wish to stay in beautiful surroundings. It was very natural too, as she was from a well to do family. She would often speak about that.

'My father loves to decorate the house and my mother has such arguments with him over this. She always says, "What is the need for all this? This sofa was very good, why change it for another new one? Why does an ordinary household need such mattresses? What paradise will you attain by hanging such expensive curtains at the doors and windows? If you saved that money you could have spent it at your daughter's wedding."' Anubha would smile wanly at this point and continue, 'My father would say, 'Do you think I haven't put money aside for your daughter's wedding? You will see how much I spend then! I will give her such fine furniture, the son-in-law will be amazed!" That was how he used to talk', then she would laugh again and say, 'Well, I did get married, but I got zero from my father.'

This time the smile was forced and bright.

I would say, 'Let that go. You will be able to get all that on your own. Your father's son-in-law will do it all; a house, a car, expensive furniture.'

She did not smile with disbelief at that nor did she speak out in despair; she would say eagerly, 'That is what I tell him too. Why won't you be able? It is humans who achieve all these things after all. What is my father? He is self-made himself. His father had nothing. He only laughs at me. But I have faith. Besides, I will do something too, although I have not achieved a BA degree. So what? There are many different jobs out there. So many doors are open to women these days.'

Unfortunately no such doors opened up for Anubha, what opened could be described as a vent at best.

She found a position as a sewing teacher at a sewing school in the neighbourhood where the pay was not worth talking about. But Anubha was happy with that; after all it was a little bit extra.

She persisted on the voyage of life floating her hopes on the strength of that 'little bit extra'. Their two airless rooms took on a magical appearance through her efforts. She had hired a fan at the beginning and the fan was followed by light cane furniture, beautifully printed curtains, mesh doored cupboards made from packing cases which had been beautified with a touch of paint, book shelves and little fancies.

Her touch imbued those ordinary things with magic and made the rooms a delightful space.

I remember that I said with a smile one day, 'You need to think of a name for this household of yours.'

Anubha said excitedly, 'Why don't you give it a name?'

I said, 'Well, it could be Happy Nest. Or House of Love'.

'The second one, the second one is lovely', Anubha said.

Amalesh smiled and said, 'Fine, I will order a signboard tomorrow and get the name written on it so that I can hang it on the door'.

Anubha said angrily, 'Signboard? Is this a shop? You are meant to say nameplate'.

'It is the same thing!' Amalesh laughed out aloud.

Amalesh had a marvellous smile.

A few days later he said with the same smile, 'No, it seems the name on the nameplate will have to be changed'.

Anubha flared up, 'When did we ever get one, now you talk of changing it?'

'But one must get the correct name on the nameplate. I think the name should be The House of Needs.'

'What do you mean?' Anubha's eyes were as round as saucers.

'The meaning is very clear. I can see that there is no end to the needs. As soon as one is fulfilled another demand takes its place.'

'But then….'

Even though the house has many needs the real culprit is the housewife and so Anubha creates a scene. She asks, 'Do you not wish to stay in a well-decorated space?'

Amalesh answers, 'Why wouldn't I? But one must stop after a point. This is neat and well decorated, so now you must want a table fan.'

Anubha's reasoning is that instead of spending money each month on the rickety rented fan with the noisy blades, they should get their own fan on monthly installments with some initial investment.

Her logic is infallible; but Amalesh feels that if she keeps increasing her list of needs and exerts all her energy on acquiring them, then when will their home ever be an abode of happiness? Why not call it Workplace or Battleground instead?

Anubha has the last word – 'That is what makes me happy!' And so at the start of each month they buy something new for their home along with the month's shopping and it is noticeable that Amalesh is the one more eager to do this.

It is clear that differences of opinion are an expression of their happiness and arguments a sign of pleasure. There is always an aura of happiness and pleasure that seems to envelop the two of them.

They lived in the two rooms downstairs for four or five years and made them into a haven. Then Amalesh got a promotion and Anubha opened a sewing school herself. This allowed them to be able to afford a south facing flat.

But they did not sever their relationship with us and would visit us whenever they had the time. A few hours would pass in laughter and talk.

I visited them too, on occasion. I saw how Anubha bought more things as time went by. They bought a fridge, a steel wardrobe, a double bed. They cooked with gas and used a pressure cooker. Amalesh used to say, 'Anu is compensating for her father's behaviour you know. She has given me nearly all the things that he should have gifted me as a father-in-law.'

Anu would retort, 'As if I have done all this on my own! I have bought these by being careful with household expenses and savings from what we have both earned.'

I would tell her, 'But that is your gift to him too. There is a lot of credit in being able to save after running a household'.

Anu would smile at her success.

I thought that their house had finally earned the name of Happy Nest. But I could also sense that a certain thirst and an emptiness was taking root in Anu behind the happy facade and the success. She had not been able to conceive a child after all these years of marriage.

One day she suddenly burst out saying, 'What was the point to doing all this? This means nothing'.

Even though I knew perfectly well what she was talking about I said lightly, 'Why, what do you now need in this house of demands?'

Amlesh gave her a little amused sidelong glance and answered, 'Now the demands are for a rocking crib and a pram.'

Anubha left the room somewhat annoyed.

After that I had to go away for a long time during which I lived in Rajasthan and a few other places. I returned only recently. I was asking Binu about all the people I had once known. The moment I mentioned Amalesh and Anubha, she mischievously said, 'Do not ask me about them! I do not want to even utter their names!'

'Why? What happened?'

'They got divorced. Do not ask for any more details. It was a real scandal.'

It took me some time to absorb this news. But why would she lie about them? I eventually came to believe her for no other reason than that. Stranger things had happened.

But today I see that she had clearly told me a lie. She had probably lost touch with them herself and muddled them up with some other couple whose marriage had broken up.

I breathed a sigh of relief when I saw them sitting side by side in the cinema hall.

I was sitting in the row behind them. Anubha had taken advantage of the darkness and her hand rested on Amalesh's lap. I smiled to myself and thought it best not to disturb their romantic time together. Besides, we would have to exchange a few words if I did speak to them. That might cause the people around me to grow annoyed and use a hundred sharp words to express their annoyance at the fact that a movie theatre was not a place for chatting to people.

I thus decided to remain quiet until after the end of the show. I would talk to them outside the hall.

The film finished eventually and once the anthem had played, I kept an eye on them as I left the show. As I stepped outside, I called, 'Anubha?'

Startled, she looked around; I called again and noticed that she began to walk away quickly without looking back.

What was going on? Had she mistaken the sound for a call from the front and was that why she was walking forward?

As a result I had to walk quickly after her and I soon caught up.

I said with a smile, 'Could you not tell where I was calling from?'

There was no response to my bright smile on her face; she said quietly, 'No, I could'.

Her face looked tired, her colour was pale and her eyes were dulled.

Was there some deeper sorrow? Had either of her parents then....I asked, 'Where are you staying these days? That same apartment or some other'.

Anubha hesitated a little before saying, 'No, the same place.'

'Then let me drop you off. Here is my car, we can chat on the way. I am back in Calcutta after such a long time. Where did Amalesh go? Which way did he go? I hope he does not hail a taxi!'

We were pushing through the crowds.

As I walked I kept an eye out for Amalesh and wondered where he was. Anubha seemed to be unconcerned.

As we got closer to my car I said urgently, 'Which way do you think he went?'

I was still worried that he would hail a taxi without knowing.

Anubha placed her hand on the car door, avoided my eyes and said in a peculiarly colourless voice, 'He went back to his own home.'

My skin prickled as I remembered what I had heard from Binu.

But what was going on then? Why were they together at the movies? What was Anubha's hand doing in Amalesh's lap under the cover of darkness?

The mystery was solved gradually. I took Anubha home

in the car. It was the south facing flat on the second floor. It still contained the bed, the wardrobe, the fridge, the gas cooker, the pressure cooker and bookshelves of a household that had once housed two people. Everything was as it had once been. But everything was covered in dust and all the things were dirty. There was only one person now instead of the two who had once lived there.

'Binu was right', Anubha said. 'We are no longer together.'

Overcome with emotion I said, 'But how is this possible Anubha?'

Anubha said softly, 'I still wonder at the same thing. And yet, it did happen.'

'But what was the reason behind such a big thing?'

'There was no reason, so we made up a reason', Anubha smiled strangely and continued, 'Just as there are laws, there are loopholes and so he pretended to be the offending party and yet it was entirely my fault'.

There was a sudden silence. We were both silent.

She spoke again in a short while, 'I had always thought of it as funny when I heard of people who were consumed by a single passion, but I saw how terrible it could be in my own case. I must have been under a spell. How shameless was my behaviour! And yet at the time, I thought that a household without children was meaningless. I had thought that he was the cause behind the absence of children. My life was unfulfilled because of his shortcomings. I began to believe in that blindly; such a cruelty took over my mind, I began complaining about everything that he did'.

Anubha smiled wanly and said, 'Perhaps you think me shameless. I admit I was. Why else would I go from doctor to doctor? He constantly said to me to not feel so bad about what I had not been given; to focus on all that I had. After all, we had each other to love and cherish. But I used to think of those words as whitewash at the time. I used to say angrily that it was convenient to try and blame a higher force for one's own faults. Let it be proved that it was my fault. You do not appear to want children and I do; so let us find out whose fault it is that we have none of our own'.

I looked at her bowed head with its parting bereft of vermilion and said, 'Let it be, talking about these things are making you sad'.

She had a certain style of wearing the vermilion in her parting, a very thin line that extended all the way from the front to the back. It covered the entire parting. But she seemed to have gone back to her maiden days.

Anubha said softly, 'It is even sadder being unable to tell anyone the truth. Under the weight of my own deeds....' she paused a little before speaking again, 'We did go to the doctor and the doctor said the fault lay in me. I did not have the ability to become a mother. When I heard the verdict, my anger and mortification drove me crazy. All the things I had said to Amalesh, all the accusations I had made seemed to ring within my heart like hammer blows.

Unable to bear the pain I took it out on him and accused him, "How hard was it to collude with the doctor? These days anyone can be bought for the right money!" When he heard that he seemed to turn to stone. Despite all the cruelty I had inflicted on him I had never seen him like that. After remaining still for a long time, he said, "What can we count on once trust is gone?"

'After that incident he stopped interacting with me; I did not know where he went, where his meals came from or when he came and left money on the table for my use. Why would I even accept those wages of anger? What would I do with it? Did my body even need nourishing? I lived on cups of tea for days. My pride had been injured as well. Was there no forgiving what I had said in anger? But instead of forgiveness, he took the road to ruin. He grew so familiar with a garrulous widow who was a student at my sewing school that tongues began wagging and it was hard to go out in public. When I expelled her from the school she threatened to expose what Amalesh had done to her. I cannot bring myself to tell you the sort of proof that she had but let me say that he took his revenge on me and proved that the fault had been mine. I went through the worst sort of despair.

'I could not imagine at the time that he would punish me in that manner but now when I think of what happened, I see that I was naïve to expect otherwise. He was a man of flesh and blood after all, and the insults I had heaped on him were perhaps responsible for goading him to the point of no return. The final straw came when the woman threatened to tell everyone about what he had done and force him into marriage; he had to admit to adultery so that we could get a divorce. After those dark days, here I am – the sewing school is doing well and so I have the means to support myself.'

'And Amalesh? What of him?' I cannot stop myself from asking.

'He is still with her. She was the only child of wealthy parents. She had taken up sewing lessons to occupy herself with something after she lost her husband suddenly at a young age. Now she is happy once again, with husband and child.'

Anubha sounded like she was summing up the solution to a mathematical problem. But to me, one part of the problem remained unsolved. Why were they at the movies together?

'Oh, that? That was purely coincidental.'

At least at the beginning Anubha continued as she talked about how she would often escape the loneliness at home by going to the movies. On one of those occasions, she found herself sitting next to none other than Amalesh. Her first reaction had been to get up and leave but then something stirred inside her and she decided to face him. She would stay till the very end of the film and see what he did.

But Amalesh gave no indication of having seen who he was sitting next to. Till the very end, when he murmured just before standing up, 'Of all the people who could have been sitting next to you…'

Anubha had been too overcome with emotion to be able to say anything.

When she got home that night she told herself that she would never go to the movies again. But a few days later in the mail, an envelope arrived with a ticket to see a show at one of the best theatres. There was a short note with it that simply asked, 'Is this really such a bad idea?'

She turned cold first and then the old anger flared up. She thought of tearing the ticket up. But then she wondered if Amalesh would explain her absence away by thinking she had not received his letter or that she was unwell. It was then that she decided to go to the show and refuse his advances to his face.

That was why she ended up going.

But when she saw how his face lit up as he saw her approaching him, she thought it would be strange to hurt him at that moment. They watched the film, wordlessly but sitting side by side.

Then it happened again; and then again.

The tickets arrived as always by mail. The letters varied a little at times.

Sometimes he wrote, 'I have heard that the film is excellent and it would be a mistake to not see it'. At other times the letter read, 'I have read two opposing reviews, we need to see which one was correct', or even, 'Your favourite actor is in this film, I have tickets to the first showing....'

It was becoming an addiction for her.

She was getting to know all the movie theatres in the city. She had seen films in both English and Bengali. When the films were being shown in locations unknown to her, the letters included instructions for her to wait near a landmark such as a bridge near her home.

On occasion they went all the way to north Calcutta to watch their films. She was less worried about being spotted by someone familiar while they were there. They sat in the most expensive seats these days. Amalesh worked in a well-paid position and could afford that.

Initially, Amalesh would drop her off at a halfway point. These days he comes all the way to the door of her house. He never enters the house though. His company has given him a car for his own use. He drives it himself and returns home late at night. He does not have to answer to anyone as a consequence.

But today?

'Today he left quickly when he saw you', Anubha said with a smile, as if talking about a small child's escapades.

I could not see her face as it was turned towards the window.

I looked at the bare nape of her neck and asked, 'But what does all this mean now? How does this all add up?'

Anubha suddenly spoke out, her voice deliberately light, 'It does not mean anything now! Nor does it amount to anything anymore! It is just a way to spend an occasional evening a little differently! That is all!'

Her face remained steadfastly turned away from me.

Selfishness
(Atmoshorbosshyo)

The Basus brought their daughter back.

They brought her back to the gentle environment in which she had once lived before her marriage. Back to her little room, where there was a single bed with snow white sheets along one wall, a book shelf and a clothes rack along another and a low table and chair on the third wall at which Shorbori had always sat down while she was studying.

Not much else fits in this room but it still seems very pleasant. Uncluttered, neat, sanctified.

Sujata had altered the appearance of the room after her daughter's marriage by depositing all the unwanted junk of the household in it. Shorbori had shared her mother's bed the few times she had come home on a visit. There was no question of having a permanent space to herself on those transient visits.

But this time she was not back for a couple of days, she was back for good. If she was not shown how elevated her position was, how would she know that even though she had come back for good, she would still be showered with the same affection as before?

How would she detect the anxious feelings that filled her mother's loving heart?

Her parents had both gone to fetch her. They brought her home from the station and said to her, 'This is your room, it is yours once again. Try to think of how you once were. The intervening days are nothing but a shadow, a dream'.

Her father's voice choked with emotion as he spoke.

Shorbori did not say a thing or shed tears, she just sat with her head bowed. The hair parting that divided her hair like a trail through a dense forest seemed to look white and stark under the electric lights. Her bowed head made the starkness more obvious. Sujata looked at that and suddenly cried out, 'I will make sure you get to remarry. I will not be able bear the sight of you like this!'

Shorbori stirred a little at this. Her appearance had not really changed a lot. She merely looked like an unmarried woman. But her mother was inconsolable.

Sujata looked at Anadi Prasad and said, 'Do not be angry with me because I am saying such things despite being my Hindu faith. She is still the maiden she used to be'.

'Angry with you?' Anadi Prasad smiled a little sadly. He then said, 'Let her rest a little. Will she eat anything?'

This time Shorbori answered him, calmly saying, 'I am not hungry Father'.

'So what? You must eat a little something', Anadi Prasad stood up. The heat on the train made him want to have a bath.

Sujata clasped her daughter's hand and said firmly, 'You will not be able to excuse yourself by saying you are not hungry. Come and eat something; you must eat with us'.

'You must eat with us!'

What did she mean by that? Was Sujata's insistence on Shorbori eating with them another indication of the inconsolable pain she was feeling as a mother?

Shorbori trembled at the thought and said quietly, 'Not today Mother'.

'All right. If you cannot manage it today, let it be. But I am telling you, I will not listen to any excuses from tomorrow. Now get changed out of these clothes you wore on the train. Have a drink of water or some tea at least.'

Shorbori pleaded, 'Let me just get some sleep now Mother. I just do not feel like anything today, I have such a headache'.

'You won't even have a little tea?'

'So late at night?'

'It is not that late. It is only nine o'clock. I am thinking, let us have some tea first; let me see what your father is doing. I wonder what that fellow Satish has done for the past two days.'

Sujata got up, a little uneasy. She had not been at home since the previous morning, who knew what had happened in the meantime.

Shorbori lay down and said, 'Give me some tea when you have made it. Can you turn the light off Mother?'

Sujata paused and asked, 'Won't you fall asleep if I turn the light off? I will bring you some tea soon.'

'You will bring the tea? Why will you bring the tea? Isn't Satish here?'

'He is here. But let me bring you the tea with my own hands....'

Sujata's words dissolve in tears as she turns the light off and leaves slowly.

Shorbori lies quietly in the darkness.

Sleep? No, sleep is far from her mind now. Her eyes are clear and dry; perhaps a little too dry. Such calmness, such a lack of tears is perhaps a little astonishing for a recently widowed woman. Even if she does not weep, she should sigh deeply at the very least.

She did not sigh once even though she was on her own. She lay there wondering instead at the fact that although her parents were so anxious about her, so eager to see her at peace, their affections did not seem to reach her heart. It was as though she stood inside a room with all the windows shut looking at the scenes outside.

Has she suffered a great bereavement then? Is that why she feels like this?

Bereavement! Shorbori tries to get to the bottom of it.

What is bereavement? The cry that rises in the core of one's heart at the loss of a loved one, isn't that bereavement? But does Shorbori feel that loss?

All she feels is a little disquiet; the emptiness of blank white walls.

Loved one? Did she love him? The man whose death they had heard of a few days ago? When did their two hearts ever unite? In actual fact, she was rather irritated at all the ceremonial grief that had needed her involvement for the past few days. Her parents went and rescued her from that. For that she was grateful to them.

What had happened to her was almost medieval. A man had severed all ties with family in a quest for freedom but his parents had brought him back home amidst tears and entreaties, thinking that marriage would be the bond that would finally secure him to life.

But it was like trying to stop the sea with a wall of sand.

The unwilling groom severed that bond once again on their first night together as easily as untying a thread from his wrist.

Despite the tragic nature of what happened, the plot was old and cliched.

She had still stayed with her in-laws for the past one

and half years. They had not spared any effort in trying to bring their son back. But it was not to be. He finally managed to escape where there was no hope of bringing him back.

A postcard with two lines of writing came from the head of his order.

Her future was decided by those two lines.

Does the inner eye grow sharper as darkness prevents us from seeing the outer world?

Shorbori tries to place herself at a distance as she thinks with that newfound clarity. Is fate as unchangeable as something carved on rock? Can one erase one's fortune and rewrite it anew? The way her mother Sujata wants to rewrite her fortunes for her?

Shorbori comes to her senses suddenly as she thinks of all this.

No, it will not do to fall to pieces, she will not allow herself to become an object of pity for others.

There is a little click in the dark, followed by a flood of light.

'Drink this tea!' Sujata requests plaintively as she turns the light on.

Shorbori sat up and said in her usual quick manner, 'Yes, and what else do you have? I suddenly realised that I am actually quite hungry'.

Sujata goes to the other room and says in a low voice, 'I don't think she is as devastated as I thought she would be, she seems to have recovered'.

Anadi Prasad says nothing, presumably because there is no answer to this.

Sujata continues to insist, 'There are all kinds of laws now, so why can we not organise a marriage for her again, tell me?'

'The Widow Remarriage Act has been law for a long time Sujata.'

'Please do not call her a widow', Sujata cries out this time.

'My heart breaks to think of it. She did not get to know what a husband is for even a day!'

She continues to sob and Anadi Prasad anxiously strokes her head and back to comfort her.

They both suffer from the same loss. Each seek solace in the other's company.

But their daughter surprised them both.

They had not hoped things to turn out this way at all.

Sujata went to ask her daughter tearfully to have dinner with them, which meant she would have to share the food that they were going to eat, certain that she would refuse to do so. Her refusal would set the scene for a suitably tragic interaction. But Shorbori laughed heartily at her mother's proposal and said, 'Please! Why start all that again? If God has seen it fit to remove obstacles from my life then I see no reason to begin with all that nonsense over fish bones again. Why don't you feed me extra milk and butter instead, that should take care of your regret'.

She also dressed in pure white as befitted a widow. When she ran out of her own sarees, she began wearing her father's dhotis instead.

She complained that her bangles jangled on her nerves, that her earrings pulled at her ear lobes and that her necklace gave her a rash. She laughed easily as she said this and gave her mother no opportunity to weep for her at all.

Sujata knew that her own heart was bound to be affected from being unable to let all the sorrow out after such a great tragedy. She said as much to those who came to visit them and offer their condolences – 'I am feeling all choked up from not being able to cry. I am terrified that my wretched daughter might fall dangerously ill after all this. It is not good to bottle up emotions like this....'

The guests would respond with a cautious, 'But there was no chance of forming any attachment. Perhaps she is not that....'

Sujata would answer regretfully, 'I understand that! But can she not see that her life is ruined forever? Can she not understand that her future is empty? Actually, she is very stoic about things'.

Needless to say, the visitors look down, unsure of what to do next.

When someone she is really close to comes to visit, Sujata quietly shares her secret wish with them. She says, 'I cannot bear to look at her in this miserable state. If I want to give her another chance at having a family of her own, will you all look down on me?'

No one says that of course. Sujata then requests them to find a groom for Shorbori, someone with liberal views and a kind heart. Helpful relatives advise them to either advertise in the papers or scan the matrimonial advertisements that are already there.

The latter happens occasionally but the advertisements are never put in the papers thanks to Anadi Prasad's ineptitude. He does not even know where the newspaper offices are, let alone the door one must enter to be able to speak to people about advertisements.

The need also seems to lessen each day. Shorbori's life does not look that empty anymore. She has filled it with laughter.

On the other hand the heart ailment that took hold of Sujata because of all the tears she never got to shed as well as those that she did seems to be growing more serious each day. Shorbori's lonely days and nights are now increasingly taken up by caring for her mother.

Days pass.

She has her mother to look after and her household chores to tend to; servants who run away and maids who leave without notice. All those blanks are soon filled by Shorbori by virtue of some unwritten inevitability.

At times the old regrets visit Sujata as she looks at her daughter's pale face. She holds her hands and says, 'This care that you are giving me, I pray that you are rewarded for this.'

She does not look for a groom anymore; these days when someone suggests it she sighs and says, 'It is not in her fate or mine! When we looked there was no one to be found; what is the point of looking now? I will not be able to do without her for one minute!'

It is true that they cannot do without her. Both parents are completely lost without her. All day they go, 'Shobu, Shobu, Shobu!' 'Where is Shobu?' 'What is she doing?'

She has to brush her younger brothers' teeth at dawn, give them breakfast and put their shoes on. She has to make poached eggs and coffee for her father. She has to chop the vegetables before cooking, put out the ingredients for the cook and give them instructions. She has to make breakfast, organise her mother's things, tidy her wardrobe, neaten her bed and fold her clothes and maintain everything in addition to attending to her mother's calls all day long, 'Shobu! Shobu!'

Anadi Prasad has become quite irritable at his wife's ill health, he cannot control his temper when he spots something wrong and frequently gives vent to his feelings. There is no telling when he will start shouting, 'Haven't you done even this? What do you do all day at home? Instead of spending twenty four hours with your nose buried in a novel, it would be good if you could look after things in the household a little!'

Shorbori quickly puts down the book she is reading and gets up.

Her brothers complain, 'Our sister did not draw lines in the exercise book for us!' 'Our sister did not fix the button on my trousers!' 'Our sister scolds us for no reason at all!'

Sujata slaps her forehead helplessly and says, 'Such is my fate! I am reduced to being an invalid at this age, or would the house be in such a state or would you be in such straits! I am eating and getting fatter, people laugh when I say I am unwell, but to tell the truth I do not have the slightest strength in my arms and legs. These people work as and when they feel like it. What can I say?'

She uses 'these' in the collective sense.

Shorbori's neat little room tires of waiting for her to come and make use of it. The dawn sun streams through the window, followed by a strong wind at midday and the golden light at day's end. Then comes the gentle breeze in the evening. It circles through the empty room like a sigh. Shorbori comes to bed almost at midnight.

By then the breeze has died down and the room has withdrawn into silence, offended by its daylong wait. It does not welcome her nor does it respond to her presence. Shorbori lies down on one side, her slight frame exhausted from her labours. Some days she falls asleep immediately and on other days, an offensive smell seems to keep sleep at bay. As she looks for the source of the smell, she remembers that her sheets have not been changed in a month. She has been waking before it is light at dawn and coming to her bed in the darkness of night – the state of the bed has escaped her notice.

She pulls the pillowcase off and flings it on the floor to try and get some sleep.

One day their man servant Satish comes to her and asks for a month of leave. He will go to his village to organise his son's marriage. He asks the young mistress first as she is the only one available. The young mistress answers him angrily, 'One whole month! Your son is going to get married over one whole month! Whatever next!'

'He won't get married straight away. I will have to look for a bride first.'

Shorbori raises her eyebrows at this, 'You haven't found him a wife yet? Then there is no hope! Enough of this discussion! Let your son find a bride first, then go and celebrate his wedding'.

Satish says somberly. 'Those city ways do not work in our village. You must give me a month off.'

'Who is supposed to do the cooking if I give you a month off? How will I make the time for that on top of all the other things that I have to do?'

'You will have to manage even if it is difficult.'

'It will not be possible! Just go if you have to! Go and stay in the village and let your son's wife take care of you! You do not have to come back. Someone else will be hired.'

Satish then took himself off to his real employers. He wept as he described to them how the young mistress had sacked him.

Sujata was about to make herself some mouth freshening

paan at the time, while she complained to her husband about the fact that she could not hope for someone to make her a paan despite having a fully grown daughter living at home. Satish burst upon this scene with his news.

'The young mistress?' Anadi Prasad answered crossly. 'The young mistress is not the one who can sack you.'

Satish said nothing as he rubbed at the corner of his eye.

Sujata asked, 'Why, what did you do wrong?'

Satish omitted certain details in the recounting of the story. He ended by saying, 'It is only in families like yours that this can go unchecked, in our society a widow in the prime of her life would do everything for the family from polishing shoes to leading the prayers! Who can afford to feed them for free from this age?'

Shorbori came in with a bowl of milk for her mother just as Satish had finished his account of the events. She waited till he was done and said sharply, 'Take your clothes and go Satish! Get out! Not a moment more in this house!'

Anadi Prasad stopped the startled Satish and said, 'Why must he go just because you have said so?'

'Of course he must! You must not stay here one moment longer Satish!'

Sujata spoke sullenly, 'What is the point of showing your temper like that! Look at your health! Who will find a new servant now?'

Strangely calm, Shorbori replied, 'No one will have to find a new servant now. I have decided I will do his share from now on. I really am letting my health go, with all this sitting around and eating coupled with lack of exercise. Satish, go. If you don't leave then I will have to find somewhere else to go.'

Satish went; Shorbori left the room afterwards.

Sujata gave her husband a frustrated look and said, 'Did you see what a temper she has?'

'Of course, I did!'

'It is my misfortune that I must put up with this kind of behavior in silence. She is so head strong, I do not think she will let Satish return to work here.'

'What can be done if she doesn't? Satish has not said anything wrong when you come to think of it. How many people in ordinary families are able to coddle their widowed daughters? What is the point of wasting valuable time reading novels rather than doing some work around the place? I am drowning in debt as it is.'

So it came to pass that Anadi was given some respite from drowning completely and Shorbori was able to preserve her health through exercise.

No wonder the saying goes; there is a reason for everything that happens.

It is said that when one of the senses is impaired, another works harder to compensate for the loss. It must be true. Sujata had lost strength in her limbs but her powers of assumption grew many fold. She was able to discover even from her bedroom on the second floor that Shorbori was not spending her afternoons in the kitchen and storeroom downstairs in an entirely friendless state. It sounded suspiciously like there were sounds of laughter and talking downstairs.

How annoying were her sons. They just had to go out together to play at that very same time. Anadi Prasad did not usually return till nightfall. Had he forgotten that the doctor had told Sujata to never exert herself by climbing up and down the stairs? Had he forgotten that they had a widow at home?

She dares not ask the question, 'Who was that downstairs with you?' but eventually one day she was moved to observe morosely, 'I think I heard laughter. Not just today, I have been hearing it a lot lately.'

Shorbori answers with her usual frankness, 'He comes frequently. It is Nontu.'

'Nontu?'

'You know him, my youngest aunt's nephew on her husband's side. Have you forgotten? He used to visit us a lot once upon a time. He has always been a great one for talking.'

'Well, if he does come here, why does he never come and see how I am upstairs?' the overriding tone in Sujata's voice is not one of sweetness.

Shorbori gives a quick smile as she answers, 'I tell him! But he claims he has a disorder of the heart that prevents him from coming upstairs!'

'But why does he come every day? What can he possibly have to talk about with you?'

Shorbori breaks into her customary peals of laughter. The laugh does not sit prettily on her worn face but it still sounds like music. Between laughs she says, 'Not everything he says means a great deal! He has always been a madcap! He says, I do not have a husband and he has never managed to find himself a wife, so the two of us should get together and tie the knot to make ourselves a family!'

Sujata forgets her heart problems and stands up in horror.

'What did you say? He said THAT to you?'

'Not for the first time today either! He says it every day!'

'How can you repeat such insulting things with a smile on your face?'

'How is it an insult?' Shorbori takes her mother by the hand and seats her down on the bed again.

'Why are you getting excited for no reason? Your heart ailment will get worse. How is this an insult? He says he feels all stirred up when he smells my cooking! And that is....'

'Really? So this was inside your heart? You go around all bare arms and white widow's weeds showing the world how virtuous you are! Did you not feel ashamed? Did you not feel any shame in repeating that scoundrel's dirty proposal? Oh Lord! So this is who you really are! And I was so trusting of you.'

'You are really making too much out of all of this! It is not as if he has asked me to elope with him. He has asked in a gentlemanly manner. What is the harm in agreeing I thought too; after all, you were looking for someone like him – with liberal views and a kind heart? Now that such a person has finally appeared….' Shorbori sits down.

Sujata fallsback against her pillow and utteres, 'Female children always turn out to be this way! Self-centred and selfish!'

Shorbori smiled gently, 'You are right mother! Not just female children though, it is the way of all the females of our species!'

Jealousy
(Eersha)

Sumanta was vigorously combing his hair with a little comb in front of the large mirror in Sujata's room. It would be better to say that he was attempting to tame it as the little comb did not seem to be making much of an impression on his thick hair. It just stroked over the surface despite Sumanta's valiant efforts.

Sujata went into the room to get candles, saw her son and said, 'What are you doing? That comb will snap! How can it possibly work on your hair?'

Sumanta went on combing his hair and answered her insolently, 'It is not your comb that I am using, is it?'

Sujata frowned, 'Great! You are certainly picking up some impeccable manners!'

Sumanta's school places a great emphasis on manners

and Sumanta has apparently also been given a certificate for this. But school rules are for school, why should he have to remember them at home? Doesn't one need open space to exercise their limbs?

Sumanta frowned even more severely than his mother and looked at her once without saying anything. He then went on combing his hair. This was a new improvement in Sumanta's behavior these days, possibly ever since he graduated to Year Eleven, but he seemed to deliberately try and ignore his parents whenever he could. What else could it be called but an improvement? Of course, his father says, 'Do not try to hide his light under a bushel Sujata! Your son is coming of age! Just wait and see how he turns out in a few more days!'

It is the general rule to refer to 'your son' in these cases.

Sujata still believes that this is a temporary change in her son. Something her son was doing in the spirit of his newly achieved grown up status. That was all it was! But something in the frown he cast at her made her smart with anger. In an attempt to exercise her maternal authority, she said a little too loudly, 'Are you going out?'

It was quite clear from his preparations that he was.

Sumanta slipped the comb into his hip pocket and said slowly and deliberately, 'Of course I am. Why, do you need something?'

He is still ready to go to the shops whenever asked. Sujata got him hooked to this by constantly sending him to the shops from when he was only around eight to ten years old.

She said sternly, 'No! You do not have to bring anything back but I still need to know where you are going.'

'What do you need to know?'

'Where are you going in the middle of a power cut and this late in the evening?'

'Why? Am I a prisoner that I must tell everyone where I am going before taking one step outside?'

'Wonderful! You are certainly picking up some great habits! Haven't you seen how your father always lets us know before leaving the house?'

'Pure slave mentality!', Sumanta throws back as he runs downstairs.

But there is nothing as shameless as a mother. And so Sujata follows him a couple of steps and raises her voice, 'Do not be too late! Take a look at the sky! It is about to rain heavily.'

She does not get an answer of course.

Back in her room she walks to the balcony and looks at the road. Sumanta is walking away fast, far enough now that she is still able to recognise him only because he is her son. The sky truly is covered in dark clouds. There is also a power cut, as inevitable as the daily appearances of the sun and the moon. But despite all that, Sujata watches her son's familiar walk and suddenly realises that both his gait and his physical appearance are like his father. He is already as tall as his father. He has already mastered the height. It was only a little while ago that he was in Year Nine. Her son is growing up too fast.

As she goes back to the room and begins closing the doors and windows, Sujata thinks to herself whether he is inheriting his father's nature as well as his physique.

His father Srimanto is such a mild, well-mannered peaceful person. He never raises his voice at anyone. Sumanta treats his father with disdain too, as he does his mother. She has often feared that Srimanto would hit his grown son in anger but no such incident has happened so far. At the most he says something quietly to himself. He says as he goes to the other room, 'Great! He is getting a good education undoubtedly. After all, it is an English medium school...'

This last remark is aimed at Sujata.

He had enrolled the boy at four in the local school that he had attended. His mother was still alive at the time. When Sujata had raised some objections over the fact that it was merely a local school, the woman had argued spiritedly, 'Why? Has my son turned out badly because he went to that school? You can count yourself lucky if your child turns out to be anything like mine!'

But Sujata had protested so much that within two years her mother-in-law had given in, saying, 'Look, just enroll your son in a missionary school; when his mother is so worried that going to a Bengali medium school will mean that her son will never get to go abroad, or get a job in Delhi or Mumbai. She might even blame you in the end – for listening to your old mother and not doing the right thing.'

She did always have a sharp and prompt way with her words.

Perhaps that was why Srimanto was so meek. He had grown up in his mother's care his entire life. She died when Sumanta had grown up a little. Sujata and her son used to joke privately about his father's excessive love for the old lady. Sujata would say, 'Your grandmother has said so? Then it is settled! Her son will not be able to do anything different!'

Sumanta would giggle at this.

Sujata had also expressed her concern at Srimanto's anxiety when his mother was ill; how would he bear it if anything happened to her?

But astonishingly, there was no great change in Srimanto when she passed away. In fact, he became even quieter if possible. The only change was his new respect for religious rituals such as praying at dawn and dusk – something he had never done before in his life. Of course this was mainly because he could not bear to see his mother's Gods neglected.

As soon as the funeral rites were over he began draping himself in one of his mother's old silk saris and going to the third floor prayer room twice a day. Sujata did not care about what he did there but she noticed a little sandalwood paste mark on his forehead when he came downstairs, just as his mother had worn. It stayed on while he ate his meal but was erased sometime before he left for work.

Sumanta used to smile some days and say, 'One of these days Father is going to become a monk, mark my words!'

Sujata agreed with her son as always, that was where she derived her strength from in any case. She had never succeeded somehow in making Srimanto 'objective' in favouring her. Even after passing away, the dead woman seemed to occupy a large part of her son's existence. And yet, she had been such a stupid rustic woman. It was quite astonishing. She would scold Srimanto if she disagreed with him, right to the end. She never let anything pass unremarked.

Srimanto's younger sister Khuku lived with her in-laws in Bhabanipur. It was not close to where they lived in Dhakuria by any means, but he still insisted on visiting her every week. If he ever missed a week, the old woman would say without hesitation, 'Perhaps you are trying to forget the fact that you have a fatherless sister, eh?'

The astounding fact was in fact the way Srimanto never spoke to her in anger and instead rushed off the very next day to see his sister, laden with all her favourite things from the shops at Gariahat – savoury snacks and sweetmeats.

His excessive respect for his mother was most likely why his weekly visits to 'Khuku's house' continued even now that their mother was dead and gone. He had told Sujata earlier that day before leaving for work, 'I think I will visit Khuku on my way home. Do not worry if I am a little late.'

'But you were there just the other day', Sujata had blurted out.

Srimanto said nothing in response and left after washing his hands and putting his shoes on. Of course, he did not frown at her like her son did.

Even though he had asked her not to worry if he was late, he wasn't late. He came back on time. He said, 'It looked like rain so I did not go there.'

As usual he draped his mother's saree and had just gone upstairs when the rain that had been threatening finally descended.

But would it have been a threat if Sumanta had been at home? If every member of a family is safely indoors, there is no greater fun than torrential rain. But the most important member of her household was still outdoors.

The more it thundered and lightning forked across the sky, the more Sujata's heart sank as she worried about her son. And within her heart she spoke to her son, 'Horrible wretch! I told you so many times not to go out, but still you had to go! Who knows where you are and how drenched you will be by the time you get home. You have only grown tall and you already think you are an adult! You are nothing but a little child! Do you remember that? You will start coughing straight away!'

She prosecutes her son in the privacy of her own mind. After all, she does not dare to say a thing to him face to face.

There is no sign of the rain abating. The thunder and lightning seem to be increasing. Amazingly Srimanto is quite at ease upstairs in his sanctuary.

Did he not feel worried at all, about what might have happened? Sujata felt it was the beginning of the end. She wanted to run upstairs and ask him, 'Are you made of stone?' But she did not have to. In a short while he came downstairs, changed into his own clothes and sat down to drink his tea. He asked, 'Has the young master not returned yet?'

Sujata erupts heatedly in an excited voice, 'Can you believe it? I told him so many times, it looks as if it will rain; do not be late – a chit of a boy and so much time outside the home! And you won't say a thing! If a thousand words from a mother do not work, one good talking to from a father will surely….'

Talking to? Srimanto touches the tea cup to his forehead in obeisance and says, 'I will give a "talking to" to that accomplished son of yours?'

He then resumes drinking his tea.

The thunder rumbles again.

Sujata tries to look out through the window but Srimanto says, 'What are you doing? The room will get flooded!'

'How can you be so complacent? What is the boy doing?'

'How strange! He is not mad that he will be wandering the streets in this weather. He must have friends who live in houses. He must be held up in one of them. Why are you worrying so much?'

This angers Sujata even more. She thinks, if the boy comes home drenched to the skin it will serve his father right. If he comes home safely, Sujata will really teach him a lesson. Why should she fear a child of his age? The only reason she does not say anything to him is because she does not want to hurt his feelings. As the hours pass, the rain lessens. The clouds quieten, the thunder ceases and the lightning stops. It continues to drizzle persistently.

A little after that Sumanta came home. He had taken a rickshaw because of the weather.

'Where were you all this time?'

'Just nearby, in Sudhamoy's house.'

Sujata had been planning all this time how she would take her son to task if he came home without getting wet. But how would she take him on? But what would he say? What if he said, 'Of course you are going to feel bad if you imagine that I have been struck by lightning! Am I a child that you must be so worried?'

Sujata said sulkily, 'Do I worry for no rhyme or reason? You might not be a child anymore but you sure do act like one. After being out in this damp wind, you will cough all night. You might say that you did not get wet but let me feel your hair. All that hair you have, let me dry it!'

Sujata tried to feel her son's hair but Sumanta shook her hand away with one movement and said, 'What do you think you are doing! There is a limit to your fussing, do you not understand!'

He dried his hair vigorously with a towel, changed his shirt and went to bed. Sujata stared in hurt silence at his back.

Srimanto stood at their son's door a little while later and smiled, 'Why go to bed hungry if you are angry with your mother?'

'Not really,' Sumanta turned on his side and said, 'Sudhamoy's mother just would not listen. She made me have dinner with them – khichri, fried eggplant and fried eggs.'

'Oh, you had a fun time then.'

'Did you hear what he said?' Srimanto said to Sujata. 'He had dinner at his friend's house. I suppose we should have our rather miserable fare of chapattis and curry as well. It is quite late.'

The power had been restored. Both the outside lights were burning. That light fell on the enormous framed portrait of Srimanto's mother that hung on the dining room wall. Srimanto looked at it in a gesture of remembrance as he did each day and began eating. At that very moment, something terrible and painful twisted inside Sujata and brought hot tears to her eyes.

She felt a great welling of jealousy within her heart for the extremely ordinary, nearly illiterate, rustic woman in the portrait.

The Steel Almirah

(Steeler Almari)

Wonderful! A fresh problem first thing in the morning! Latika lashed out. She had been about to say disaster, but she quickly changed it to problem.

Then she came to the room where Poritosh sat and said in the same tone, 'Listen to the good news of the day! Your much loved elder brother has come to visit us, all the way from your precious Nayanpur.'

Poritosh had just taken a sip from the tea cup in his hands. He was watching the window keenly as he waited for his morning papers to make an appearance.

As their rooms were on the ground floor, the paper boy threw it in through the window each morning.

'My elder brother from Nayanpur?' Poritosh spilled some of the tea in surprise.

Latika's sarcasm stems from the knowledge that once upon a time this older cousin was rather dear to Poritosh.

But then she is always sarcastic when the subject of discussion is Nayanpur no matter who the person might be.

Apparently, the experiences she had a long time ago when she stayed for a few days as a newly married bride in the ancestral home in Nayanpur were more than enough. Judging from her comments since that time, the stay had not been pleasant at all.

But what had happened to her?

What could have embittered her for the rest of her life?

It was actually something quite unimportant. The main reason was the depth of Poritosh's affection for that obscure village. She knew of his feelings each time she began criticising the rustic place in no uncertain terms. His love was evident in every line of his face.

Her hatred was almost like that she might feel for another woman trying to come between Poritosh and herself.

It was not as if Poritosh did not know that. That was precisely why he had been forced to bury his love for his roots in the deepest recesses of his heart and had gradually forgotten that it had once existed. It was well and truly buried by now.

There was no point in needling Poritosh by saying 'Your beloved elder brother' any more. How many times in a year did Poritosh think of him these days any way?

Even letters asking after each other's wellbeing had grown infrequent. The only time he wrote these days was when he sent a festive greeting with the all inclusive phrase 'I hope you are all well'.

This is a very neat turn of phrase. When one queries how the others are in a letter, there is an invitation for an answer. That indicates the chance of further interactions.

But what a fine thing it is to say 'I hope…!' There need not be any expectation of receiving an answer.

This relegates even the closest among our relatives to an annual offering of wishes. Poritosh had the same degree of contact with his elder brother.

Thus his brother's arrival had truly come out of the blue. That was why Poritosh spilled his tea.

His throat dry, he managed to somehow say, 'Borda? He came from Nayanpur this early?'

Latika smirked and said, 'How should I know? I haven't memorised the trains that come and go from Nayanpur, have I?'

Poritosh finished his tea quickly, put his cup down and asked, 'Haven't you talked to him yet?'

'Why would I be so eager to go and greet him? The maid came and told me', Latika smirked again.

The room where Poritosh had been drinking his tea was a storeroom, but it had a table and the tea things.

There is a good room near the front door which Latika had set up as a drawing room. The house needed at least

one room where guests and outsiders could be taken to.

There was a television, book shelves and a lot of knickknacks in that room. But the stupid maid had made Borda take a seat there like an outsider and then come in to announce his arrival. But why wouldn't she? The moment she heard that the guest was the master's brother, she knew she had to show him respect.

Poritosh said feebly, 'I wonder what happened to make him to come this early and that too unannounced?'

Why else?

Latika pulled her usual face and said, 'He will talk himself dry before bringing up the real reason – getting some money off you. You will hear about how it is hard to survive in the village these days. There are no crops in the field, no fish in the river and no thatch on the roof. You will hear all that!'

It was not as if Poritosh found her words particularly soothing but he did not protest immediately either.

He only tried to recall when the last time had been that his brother had come with the aim of extracting some money from him. Did those words even match the memories he had of a tall man with an easy laugh?

But on the other hand he could not bring himself to say to Latika, 'When has my brother ever come to me for money?' No, he could not.

WHO knows what unwritten rules had rendered Poritosh incapable of telling Latika the truth? At all times.

When the maid's daughter Rekha comes to announce that her mother will not be coming in and Latika says without a second thought, 'Do not simply give me this news and run home. Do the dishes that have been waiting for your mother's attention!'

Can Poritosh not say, 'How strange! That little girl who is clearly younger than our own daughter, will she be able to do all those dishes?'

The most he can manage is, 'Will you be happy with the work she does?'

But Latika knows exactly what he means. As the saying goes, a snake catcher knows everything about a snake; even the sound of its sneeze.

And so she says heatedly, 'I will deal with it! Do you think she will get to leave this house until I am satisfied with her work?'

Or when Poritosh's friends and family visit and Latika says, 'Tea? No, I cannot make tea now! I will get the maid to bring some sweets from the shop and serve it with some cold water from the fridge!'

Poritosh never dares to say, 'But you seem to make tea for yourself all the time! Just because it is my friend who is here....'

He does not dare do anything of the sort.

When Latika does do something voluntarily, he is

overcome with gratitude and praises her good sense and attention to detail repeatedly.

That is why he cannot not retort back at her now, 'When has my brother ever come to me for money?'

No one knows why Poritosh always acts so guilty all the time; like an intruder in his own home.

Especially when Nayanpur is involved in some way.

But he still has to summon up courage and once he is able to, he says to Latika, pouring sympathy into his words, 'Well, if he is here now, it means more work for you, right? We cannot let him go without feeding him , on top of which you have run out of gas in the last few days, haven't you?'

Latika gives him a smile laced with sarcasm and says, 'Does it matter if I run out of gas or breath! When it is your brother from the country home, one must organise a full banquet for him!'

Bhobotosh is waiting in another part of the house.

Poritosh is actually feeling quite excited about his guest. But he cannot go to greet him without fully comprehending Latika's mood. He might end up sitting down for a good chat, only to find that Latika has decided to serve his brother a few snacks bought from the shops.

Village folk view food bought from shops in the city with suspicion as well as pity.

When his brother visited them in the past, he always came by the midday train, stayed the afternoon and left at night.

Did Poritosh ever say to him forcefully, 'Why not stay the night at least? We will talk all night about old times and you can leave in the morning.'

Poritosh Bhattacharya, mid-ranking officer in a government office, has never been able to find the conviction to talk like that. He has only thought about it.

Despite his strongest desires he could not even say to Latika, 'Why not fry a couple of luchis for him? He worries about eating too much of this shop-bought food!'

Those things have to stay unsaid.

Bhobotosh picks up the plate filled with snacks and says, 'This is one strange custom you city folk have! You just don't feel that you have shown enough hospitality unless you have spent a lot of money on a whole bunch of snacks in a shop. If your wife had given me a couple of rotis from your meal instead to have with my tea, I would have eaten that happily. This stuff is only going to give me indigestion!'

Poritosh does not need to look at Latika to imagine the sour look clouding her face at that moment.

He tries to change the mood in the room by quickly asking, 'Indigestion and you? Weren't you once able to digest iron bars for breakfast?'

Bhobotosh laughs uproariously. He says, 'Once upon a time!' Which means that was all in the past. 'Not any more, brother! Once I could also bend an iron rod with my bare hands. I could swim from one bank of the Ganges to the other. Now you will find neither Rama nor his city of Ayodhya. The Ganges is in such a state that I do not feel like having a swim there anymore.'

TRULY, once he had been like the great king Rama in the city of Ayodhya.

He had been the hero of his neighbourhood. He had started a library in the village, begun a gymnastics club and a football team. He had been the first to help others whenever there was a need.

Poritosh had held on to the bright memories of those days in his heart for a long time. But now things had changed for the country and those days of simple pleasures were long gone.

Poritosh has changed as well. He does not hold those values as dear anymore.

Despite all the changes, Paritosh still feels uneasy when his Borda visits. He does not want anything to spoil the time that Bhobotosh spends with them.

Of course, Latika is not so rude as to insult an elder with her words. She never says anything before he has barely walked out across the threshold, 'All that fuss over what we got from the markets! Why, he ate everything all the same!'

Even just now, when she asked whether it mattered if she ran out of gas or breath, she did not say it so loudly that it would reach the ears of anyone in the sitting room.

Poritosh is always soft spoken. His words cannot be heard outside the room he is in. He now speaks anxiously in that tone, 'Do you really have to make a lot of items? Just give him the same things we eat.'

'You are saying that now, but later you will be the one fretting about what I did not do – the one saying to me that I should have made some eggplant fritters! You will go on about how your brother prefers the fritters and so on.'

'No, no! You do not have to do any of that! I will just let him know that our gas has run out.'

'All right! And please, for heaven's sake, do not rush to the shops to buy fresh fish. Last time he took a look at the fish in the fridge, wrinkled his nose and said – you spent good money on this stale fish! I know you must adopt city ways as soon as you move to the city. Otherwise it is hard to save face – what a twisted smile he had as he said those things.'

Even though he could not imagine his brother smiling in that fashion, Poritosh says nothing as usual and lets her words pass. He says, 'Yes, I am going.'

The maid comes and looks at them. She said, 'What is happening aunt? Your relative asked me if I had not informed you of his arrival. He said - what need of informing them anyway, I am family after all – let us go inside.'

She swallows a little and continues, 'But I did not want him to walk in unannounced, so I told him that the master was in the bathroom and that you were doing your prayers.'

'Prayers?'

Latika laughs as she said, 'You have learnt to tell tales quite well! Thank God you did not say I was meditating! But you did well!'

The maid replies glumly, 'What could I do anyway? A relative has come all the way from the village and is waiting outside. Yet you people seem unwilling to go and see him!'

The happiness Latika had just felt at the maid's clever ploy seems to evaporate as soon as she hears the woman say this. The working classes are getting too big for their boots these days!

Poritosh quickly says 'Yes, I am going to him.'

Latika lowers her voice and says, 'Be strict from the very start. He will definitely feel jealous once he sees the television in that room. He will think his brother has become very wealthy. Be sure to mention how expensive everything is in Calcutta. Do not forget to tell him how we are paying for the television in instalments in the course of your conversation. I know how you feel guilty about living in comfort. As if you have stolen these things from someone else. I see it in your behavior all the time!'

Poritosh thinks that it was his fate to feel guilty about everything anyway. But he keeps quiet as usual.

Latika has finished what she has been saying by then, 'You have rights to the produce of the land and the fish from the ponds back in the country, but are you getting anything though? It is all going towards feeding them....'

'That is true,' Poritosh stops her from saying anything further with his remark and goes to the other room.

He found Bhobotosh studying the road from the window.

In a way it was a relief that he did not have to face the person whom they had left waiting for this long.

He called from behind, 'Borda, how did you get here at this hour? Which train did you catch?'

Bhobotosh turned to look at him and said in his booming voice, 'You are surprised, aren't you? A really convenient bus service has started in Nayanpur. It is actually meant for the market folk but the fellows take on an extra passenger or two if they know you. It starts from there at five in the morning and gets to Esplanade here by half past six.'

Poritosh had already bent down to touch his feet to show respect and Bhobotosh had given him a hug saying, 'Let it be! Let it be!'

He might not have the good health and strength of the past but the framework was still the same. Poritosh barely came up to his brother's chin when enfolded in his arms.

After he had released Poritosh, Bhobotosh continued with what he had been saying.

'Since the bus service began, I have been planning to pick a Sunday and make this trip. In the cool of the morning – but you never write letters, you have always been a lazy sod! Tell me, how are you? I have not seen you for such a long time!'

Poritosh said, 'As well as can be expected. You are far better off where you are. Calcutta is not the best place to be in these days.'

'We are better off?'

Bhobotosh laughed loudly again. 'I suppose so! You know how they say that each bank of the river always thinks the other side is doing better? You are saying we are better off and we think the same about you.'

He did not seem to have noticed the well decorated room and its television set as he said this.

'The Nayanpur you knew as a child is no longer there. Nayanpur and its neighbouring Jhamot and Badu are all on the way to being ruined. Politics has destroyed the villages and turned the people into animals. Everyone is out to profit for themselves. On one hand you have the land reforms of Operation Barga and on the other is local government or the Gram Panchayat – each siding with political parties, there is no peace any more. The bigwigs push their agendas and the police turn a blind eye to everything. Do you remember Dinu Keertoni? The woman used to sing, "The king's daughter Pari, whatever she does is all right", this is the same situation.'

What was Poritosh supposed to say to this? He changed the topic and said, 'What news of your school?'

'Alas! You do not know then! They made me retire

about six months ago when I turned sixty. Do you know what the rules are like these days? If they cannot do any good, they will definitely do some harm. On one hand the walls of the ancient classrooms are collapsing from lack of maintenance and the classes flood when it rains, I complained so many times but to no avail; the authorities do not care about that stuff. On the other hand, they pass a rule that older teachers would not be retained, therefore sack them. Apparently, one loses mental acuity at sixty. But remember our teacher Shyambabu? He taught with success till he was seventy. What teaching! It still gives me a thrill when I think about his lessons! He taught from the days when the school was first started. All these rules had not been invented at the time.

Bhobotosh gets quite excited as he continues.

'What if the voters suddenly decided one day that all old ministers would have to go? How many of you would last, I ask? Each and every one of them is a doddering old man, clinging to power, gasping for life as they stand for re-election! As if they do not lose mental sharpness when they turn older, as if they are the Chosen few. The real reason behind creating these rules is to empty posts that can then be given to their pet nominees. Anyway, good riddance to all of that! The situation was gradually becoming such that it was hard to maintain self- respect and keep working. But Nayanpur High School is on its last legs. If teachers decide that their duty is to teach students about party politics, then what better can one expect?'

This is the way he talks when the topic is one dear to his heart. It is as though he has his opposition in front of him. But what of the one who is there in front of him. Are these words affecting him at all?

Not really, He is still reeling under the assault of the words he heard a little while ago, his ears had stopped taking anything in. The words are hammering at his senses – 'made me retire about six months ago.'

That means Latika's guess was correct.

What now? How to extricate himself from the situation?

Latika enters the room at this point. She has a cup of tea in one hand and a plate with two little sweets and two biscuits in the other.

She lowers the plate carefully on to the centerpiece, touches the visitor's feet and asks, 'I hope you are well?'

Her face is like the morning sun.

Poritosh stares at that face.

Latika goes on, 'The gas in the kitchen has run out, that was why it took so long to make you some tea. You do not like outside food, so I only brought these for you to eat. I made the tea on the Primus stove. Today's lunch will have to be cooked on a clay oven.'

Bhobotosh says quickly, 'That is quite alright! This is enough for me!'

He does not say anything about the clay oven most probably because he has no idea that lighting it is a difficult task.

Latika does another unbelievable thing. She looks at Poritosh and said, 'You have a day off. Go to the markets and see if you can buy some good fresh fish. Your brother does not really like fish that has been kept in the fridge. It will be great if you can get some hilsa. Of course, it will not be less than sixty rupees a kilo. But so what, I do not think one can get hilsa in Nayanpur. We can eat some hilsa too, in his honour!'

Bhobotosh says agitatedly, 'No, no! You do not have to do all that for me! To be honest, I ....'

Latika says, 'Not at all! You have visited us after such a long time.....'

Was Poritosh dreaming? It must have been that! Why else could he still hear Latika saying, 'Yes, a good spinach dish with hilsa head! How long has it been since we last had it? Brother, do you not like spinach with hilsa head?'

'Of course, I love it! But where do I find it? Our house has spinach growing all around it but hilsa? I had forgotten all about it. Nayanpur has truly become rundown these days. But it is available where you are, Poritosh – when your wife loves it so much.'

The Said brother's wife speaks up in a complaining tone, 'Can you speak to your brother about that? He is becoming more miserly each day....'

Poritosh sighs, 'Of course, I am. As if you do not know the state of the markets? What can I say, only God knows how I manage to maintain my household! This television that your sister-in-law wanted so much, the payments for it have meant that I had to cut spending on other things. Examination fees are due for both the boys. I do not know how I am supposed to find the money for that.'

Poritosh feels quite satisfied with himself. At least Latika will not be able to say that he was weak.

Bhobotosh seem to remember something when the boys are mentioned. He asks, 'Of course! Where are they? Not one have I seen so far.'

Poritosh looks around as if searching for them and says, 'I do not think they are awake yet....'

'What? Not awake yet? Sleeping till this late – very bad! Now is not the time for bad habits.'

Poritosh tries to salvage the situation by saying, 'Actually, it is because it is Sunday. They stayed up studying till late and slept in.'

Bhobotosh says loudly, 'That may be, but do wake them up. My father used to say sleeping on after the sun rose decreased one's lifespan. So, what examinations are they studying for?'

'Shubho and Dhrubo are both sitting the school finals. Shubho was held back one year and that is why'

Latika snarls, 'He did not do it on purpose. He had been unwell!'

'Yes, yes! And Tukai has tests every day.'

'Really? Has she grown up so much as well? Call them please. I am in a bit of a rush....'

Rush? This is good news! Latika thinks, and perhaps so does Poritosh; in the hopes of not having to entertain their guest all day long.

Poritosh can imagine the sullen look on Latika's face and the sarcastic, pitying smiles on her children's lips coupled with annoyance; looks that he had observed on previous occasions.

It was also a mystery as to why Latika was being so respectful and generous. Poritosh would only be able to relax once his brother had left without any further incident.

After all this was not a visit from her brother, the one who was in the army; the one whose visits meant the whole house coming to life. Latika would be grateful and her children would be overwhelmed by stories of his exploits while the kitchen would hum to the sounds and smells of a feast worthy of a hero. No, this was Poritosh's rustic brother.

Poritosh still said faintly, 'What do you mean by hurry? Won't you have lunch before you go?'

Bhobotosh sounded regretful, 'That is the problem. My sister-in-law continually writes to us asking why I do not visit them. This time she has extracted a promise that I must have a meal there if I am in the city. If I do not go, my wife will be very upset. There is another reason for going there of course. Your sister-in-law, my wife has asked me to do something – hello? You have all only just woken up? It is far better to wake early and study than study till late into the night. The brain is more alert at dawn. I was telling your mother how my father used to say that it reduced your life if you slept on after the sun was up. And you, my little Lakshmi, come to your uncle! Look at how tall you are!'

Their children had come to the room and were standing there, yawning widely and rubbing their eyes.

Poritosh had hoped that Latika would indicate to them to touch their uncle's feet. But his wish was not fulfilled. He saw that she too yawned, perhaps in relief.

The children stood there stupidly for a few seconds and then suddenly turned around and trooped out through the door.

Their drooping pyjamas and slack cords were a sight to behold. How did they manage to walk away without tripping and falling?

Latika stood up and said in a voice dripping with reproach, 'Then you are not staying after all? I had hoped we would have a good meal today in your honour. But it seems that is not to be. Will you have some more tea?'

Bhobotosh said, 'No, too much tea does not sit well with me.'

Latika went inside with a light heart. Would Bhobotosh make any demands on his brother when they were alone together? She did not think so.

But Latika was wrong. Bhobotosh did ask for something. He held his brother's hands in his and said with suppressed emotion, 'You must listen to a request I will make!'

He reached inside his coarse cotton shirt, brought out a wad of notes from an inner pocket and said in a deeply mortified voice, 'You must keep this.'

There were about eight hundred rupees in the bundle.

He tried to force it all into Poritosh's hands.

Astounded, Poritosh asked, 'What do you mean, I keep these?'

Bhobotosh was back to normal. He said quite easily, 'Keep means keep. What else should it mean?'

Poritosh asked incredulously once again, 'And then?'

Bhobotosh laughed uproariously.

'What do you think? I want you to spend it of course.'

'You want me to spend your money after you have given it to me for safekeeping?'

'How strange! What is all this talk about whose money it is? Money is for spending where it is needed.'

Poritosh asked, 'Did you bring this money today to give to me?'

'No! I came with the idea of spending it on a frivolous matter – but that is of little consequence. Take it and put it away. I know how easy it is to feel a loss of pride in such things!'

Bhobotosh had come to Calcutta to with eight hundred rupees to spend it on a frivolous matter? That was hard for Poritosh to accept.

'So, what is this frivolous matter you were going to spend this money on?'

'What can I say? Your sister-in-law's sister has a son

who has set up a steel furniture shop after being unable to find a job. As soon as your sister-in-law hears of this, she just happened to remember that she has always had a wish for a steel cabinet with a locker all her life. Imagine! She never says a word to me about this in her entire life but the moment her nephew gets himself a shop, she wants one! Apparently he has promised her a good price. Who falls for that kind of pitch? He will probably fleece her especially on account of her being his aunt! I know how these fellows play their tricks! Then I thought again and felt that since I had a bit of money saved up from when I retired, why not get her what she has always wanted?'

Poritosh said somberly, 'Forgive me, but I could not possibly take your money.'

'Forgive you! That means you do not think of me as family!'

Bhobotosh sounded hurt.

Poritosh said brokenly, 'But you said she has wanted it for a long time....'

'Let it be! Who can make sense of what women want. Is there any logic behind such wishes? A lifelong school master's house with two old people rattling around in it, what treasures do we own that we must store them in a steel cabinet with a locker? We have this here, this is where we should store things that we truly value any way.'

Bhobotosh slapped his chest with a broad smile.

'Borda?'

'What is this again? Listen to you, calling me Borda in that tone just like when you were a child! Look, you have real needs – examination fees, all these worries – how can your sister-in-law's steel cabinet be more important than all of that to me?'

The Transalator

This is a book of short stories by Ashapurna Devi. They have been translated from their original Bengali into English by Ruma Chakravarti.

Ruma has been blogging about Bengali literature for seven years, translating songs, poems and stories. A year after she started, three volumes of Ruma's translations of Tagore's work were published at the Kolkata Book Fair in 2013. Ruma credits her love of the Bengali language to her schooling and her parents.

Ruma translates from Bengali to English in order to make more people aware of the rich body of Bengali literature, which remains relatively unknown to English-speaking readers when compared to other languages to which the Nobel Prize in Literature has been awarded. Her style of translating has been praised widely and is remarkable for the intimate experience it offers the readers. Ruma feels that translation literature as a genre benefits the growing numbers of diaspora children and young adults who wish to revisit the stories their parents grew up with.

The writer she has chosen for this book is Ashapurna Devi, a popular author. The stories have been selected to provide a look at human issues such as rural migration, feminism and the refugee experience.

Ruma was born in Ghana and schooled in India. After living in Africa, India and Papua New Guinea, she now calls Australia home. Growing up in two countries herself and as a mother of bilingual children, Ruma feels that translated literature is one of the things that can help people across the world to understand each other better.